MARK 1

STONEKICKER

To Paul,

I'll use the nickname Carpets in the next one!

Cheers
Mark

Copyright © Mark Romanow 2011

Mark Romanow has asserted his right under the Copyright, Designs and Patents Act 1988 to be identified as the author of this work.

ISBN 9781460950722

Dedicated to
Eleanor and Olivia

With thanks to my Dad for all his help,
Pat Winslow for her advice and my wife Heather for her tolerance.

Chapter 1

This is not a tale of redemption or heroism.

I didn't start out bad. Badness just seemed to grow on me. It was like this bit of fungus I had growing on my big toe when I was small. It was tiny initially but seemed to develop into something quite large and unpleasant without me really noticing. I guess it was a result of neglect and the filth that was ever-present in my environment. At times I would become aware of it and feel such a sense of revulsion I had to quickly think of something else. One time though, I tried to cut it out. As soon as the knife cut into it I screamed. It had become a part of me. I felt I was going to lose my mind but my mother brought me a bag of my favourite crisps and I calmed down and I almost forgot all about it. Eventually it just dried up and fell off and it looked as if it had never been there in the first place. But I always remembered it and washed my feet properly every day for the rest of my life.

My parents were both in their teens when they married. I was only about two years old at the time and wasn't invited. In the few years that they were together it was usually my father's job to drive me to school. He had a bright red sports car which, to an easily impressed five year old, was the epitome of all that was cool. He would often drive me to school then tell me to wait in the car for five minutes while he went inside. He would return and tell me that I didn't have to go to school that day because I was ill. After the initial confusion this would please me no end. My studies in the art of deception began at an early age.

On one such day he reversed out of a parking space in the school car park and hit a parked car.

"Fuck! Fuck! Fuck! Fuck!" he shouted and performed

a spectacular smoking wheel-spin before flying out of the car park. The G forces flung my head back into the seat. His head spun round as he scanned for witnesses.

"You didn't see any of that," he said.

Sometimes we would be in the bread van that he drove for work. These days were my favourite ones because I would get nice cakes from the factories we'd visit on his rounds. Other days he would take me to the shop and buy me some sweets and a comic before driving to the house of some salacious young scantily clad woman. After a very brief introduction the woman would set me up in front of the TV while they went upstairs 'for a chat'. Eventually he would come down looking a bit hot and bothered and we would leave. He always smelled nicer when he came downstairs. Before taking me home he would always eat a banana as he believed that this was the best way to mask his cigarette breath. I never really understood these rituals but he knew I liked skiving off school with my sweets and comics so his secrets were safe. I never knew why he took me with him on his liaisons; I guess it was just some sort of strange father/son bonding session. But I learnt a lot during these trips. Although I kept his secrets, I didn't believe that what he did was wrong. The women were very nice to me and my father was always kind and generous, so all in all I quite enjoyed it.

Whenever we were at home there would invariably be rows about money, work and women and my father's blind determination to acquire all three. Good food was always scarce due to his inability to acquire the former. My mother's way of dealing with this was to provide a wholesome cheap meal by producing copious amounts of homemade cauliflower cheese. I hated cauliflower cheese.

My father's entrepreneurial skills never really came

to fruition during his marriage to my mother. He was frequently coming up with ideas for new business ventures which just about kept our heads above water but never really took off. He didn't like working for other people and whenever he did it never lasted. He would always quit, blaming the bosses who 'didn't have a fucking clue' and 'couldn't organise a piss-up in a brewery'. I kept my distance from him on those days. It irked me that the rest of the world was full of these horrid people. My father knew everything. Why wouldn't people recognise that and give him a great job with loads of money?

My favourite times were the weekends. On Friday nights my father would go to the local pub. My brother and I would be sent to bed and, under instructions from my mother, I would tell my brother a story to send him to sleep. These were usually variations on familiar fairy tales where the protagonist invariably ended up being eaten alive by wolves, bears or witches. He didn't like them but eventually went to sleep. As soon as I was confident that he wasn't going to wake up I would sneak down to the living room where my mother let me curl up in front of the television to watch the late night horror film. My father would usually get back from the pub just in time for the film to start having bought me a bottle of cola and a hot meat and potato pie from the off-licence at the end of the pub. As they sat puffing away on their fags I would squeeze between them and fill my face while being gleefully terrified by the horror film. I had the occasional nightmare afterwards but I daren't tell my mother in case she stopped me from having this marvellous treat. My parents would make me swear on not to tell my brother or risk losing the privilege.

The monsters I had thus far encountered were all make-believe and fantastical. The real ones hadn't shown their faces. Yet.

Chapter 2

When I was nine years old I went to live with my maternal grandmother and my blind step-grandfather in Brighton. Alone, I got on the train, waved goodbye to my mother, travelled to London, got on the underground to Victoria Station and boarded the train to Brighton. It was one of those old fashioned trains which had small glass doored carriages coming off the walkways. I managed to get one all to myself and sat by the window watching the world go by. As the train was about to leave a rather dishevelled looking old man entered the carriage and, although there were five empty seats, silently sat next to me. He immediately put his head on my shoulder and went to sleep. It was starting to get dark and as we were leaving London I could see into the brightly lit houses that we passed. As I tried to ignore my new companion I gazed at families eating dinners, people in their kitchens, living rooms and bedrooms. I tried to imagine what their lives were like, wondering if they were happier than me. I doubted it. As the train was about to go under a bridge I noticed the legend daubed on its side in bright orange informing me that Mike Humphrey was a twat. I wished that my presence in the world could instil such passion in a person that they might risk their lives to make such a statement about me.

The train eventually arrived at Brighton. I slid out of my seat, causing the old man to bang his head on the window and swear at me. When I got off the train it was dark but I could still hear the occasional gull screeching angrily in the night. I deeply inhaled the smell of the sea and thought about how lucky I was to have such an adventurous life. There was no-one there to meet me, but I knew where I was going so I was alright.

My grandmother worked long hours as a waitress and would invariably leave the old man with me after school. He had never liked his wife's family, acknowledging our heritage by always referring to us as Irish/Polish gypsies who ate him out of house and home. He took great umbrage at my being there and never called me by my name. For that year I almost thought my name was 'fucking glutton'. Needless to say I wasn't the most accommodating grandson. Whenever I was alone with him, at some point he would ask me to take him to the toilet or ask me to make him a sandwich and a cup of tea. I would sit as still and quiet as possible, knowing he couldn't see me. He would swear under his breath and eventually wet himself to punish my grandmother. There was no way he was as incapable as he made out and I just wasn't prepared to jump whenever he clicked his fingers, as my grandma did. He never expressed gratitude towards her for the things she did and would always swear at her calling her a 'mad old bitch'. When he wasn't being abusive he would just sit in his armchair asleep, with his bottom set of false teeth protruding from his mouth and a handkerchief stuffed behind his glasses. Why he wore glasses I never knew.

In her own way my grandmother did get her own back on the old man, although I felt that it was just through being herself rather than by calculating acts of revenge. One day we all went to the shops. She was one of those people who just wanted to get from A to B in as short a time as possible. She had hold of the old man's arm and I trailed behind. With tunnel vision she marched ahead, never telling him where the kerbs were. He stumbled and fell at least a dozen times by the time we got to the shopping centre.

"Slow down, you mad old cow," he shouted. "I'm blind!"

"Stop showing off and get up," she replied and continued onwards without altering her pace or showing any concern for him.

We arrived at the shopping centre and she walked up to a young man and grabbed him firmly by the arm. He swung around in alarm.

"Excuse me dear," she said in a simpering pathetic tone. "Could you help me find the Home Stores? My husband's blind, you see."

"Oh, er, yeah, OK," said the man in a state of bewilderment. My grandmother didn't release her vice-like grip on him until we got there. I dropped further back.

"Do you want to come in with me?" she asked me. "I need to get some new tights and some ciggies."

"No. I'll pop and have a look in the comic-book shop, if that's alright," I said.

"Alright then, meet me back here in ten minutes." She gave me twenty pence. "Treat yourself." That's more like it, I thought. She let go of my step-grandfather and walked into the shop.

"Annie!" he shouted. "Annie! Where are you?" He started to whirl around in a circle waving his stick in the air. I watched with bemused interest from a distance. "Annie! Me legs is gone. Come back!" He started staggering dramatically until a woman walking by ran to help him. As soon as she reached him, he collapsed onto the pavement. Quite a crowd was forming around him now. I went and found the comic shop.

By the time I came out the police had arrived at the scene. The old man was lying on the pavement crying now and refusing to get up when they tried to help him. I kept my distance. Eventually my grandmother strolled out of the shop. She spotted the commotion and marched through the crowd. She grabbed the old man by the arm.

"Get up Sid!" she said and dragged him to his feet. "I'm very sorry my dear," she said to the policeman. "He's blind and senile. You don't know how difficult it is for me. I did leave him with my grandson but he seems to have gone." I couldn't believe my ears. She spotted me. "Oh there he is. Come here now," she called to me. "What do you think you're doing, leaving your poor granddad on his own?" She looked at the policeman and raised her eyebrows. "Boys eh!"

"He's not my granddad," I muttered as we left the crowd and headed home.

They lived in a small, one-bedroomed flat and I had to sleep on the bedroom floor in a sleeping bag. Every night without fail the old man would climb out of bed, reach for his 'piss-pot' which he kept by the side of the bed, and stand there for about ten minutes relieving himself. He would follow this with an enormous fart before climbing back into bed. His aim was not always straight and I would occasionally get splashed. Eventually I got fed up with this. I decided to start hiding his pot on top of the wardrobe. I would take great pleasure in watching him, clad only in a white string vest, crawl around the floor on his hands and knees searching for the pot, all the while swearing.

"Where's my fucking bucket?" he would mutter. He would eventually give up and crawl out of the bedroom to find the toilet. My grandmother, being hard of hearing, would be oblivious.

One morning I was running late for school. I ran into the bathroom and brushed my teeth. Halfway through I stopped. There was a horrible taste in my mouth. I looked down at the tube of toothpaste. To my horror I saw that it wasn't toothpaste but my step-grandfather's haemorrhoid cream. The tubes were virtually identical. This one had bloody smears on it. I had once barged into the bathroom and caught him applying the ointment. He stood there wearing only a string vest with his right hand smearing the ointment up his backside. This memory flooded back and I threw up in the sink.

The next morning the old man asked me to take him to the toilet. This involved me walking in front with him holding on to my shoulders as if we were doing the conga.

"Pass me my cream," he said and dropped his baggy Y-fronts. I picked up the toothpaste tube, handed it to him and walked out. The cry he emitted a minute later implied that toothpaste on a sore bum was probably a more unpleasant experience than brushing one's teeth with haemorrhoid cream. I watched as my grandmother ran in to help him, washing his backside with a wet flannel before folding it neatly and putting it on the side of the sink. I made a mental note never to use a flannel in that house ever again.

I eventually grew tired of playing these games with the old man, and as soon as my grandmother left for work I would climb out of the window (I wasn't allowed a key) and make my way down to the beach, whatever the weather. Anything to get away from him.

The seaside in winter was especially magical. There were no crowds and I would wander down the promenade looking out across the sea, imagining myself on a ship in the storm being assaulted by the spray and the rain as I struggled not to be thrown overboard. I would walk through the West Pier wishing I could afford to have a go on the Victorian amusements. The fortune telling and 'what the butler saw' machines were particular favourites. I would scan the metal trays under each machine searching for coins.

Whenever I had any money I would buy myself some cockles and stand at the end of the pier braving the elements, looking down through the gaps in the rotting floorboards at the waves hitting the legs of the structure, sure that at any moment they would buckle under the strain and I would be plunged into the icy depths below.

On the walk back home I would always stop outside a shop that sold glass ornaments and look inside. It was owned by an old man who could always be seen on his chair in the window blowing glass. He would hold a glass tube over a flame and create the most breathtakingly beautiful ornaments. There were fairytale carriages and unicorns in the window, sharing the shelves with sea horses, parrots and bears. After a while the old man would acknowledge my presence with a slight nod. This made my day and I would dutifully nod back like a grown-up. I saved up my pocket money for about six months and eventually built up the courage to walk into the shop. He put down his tools and came to the counter to ask what I would like. The ornaments were quite dear but I'd seen a small glass animal that I could afford. I think it might have been a dog, but I liked to think it was a wild wolf. On the walk home one of its legs broke off in my pocket but it was still my most prized possession. The fact that it was now lame only endeared it to me all the more. I kept it on the floor under the dresser in the bedroom. From my prone position in my sleeping bag I could look at it glistening in the moonlight before I went to sleep. I would imagine wandering through snowy mountain forests with the wolf at my side protecting me from the predators. I dreamt about lying in a dark cave with the wolf on top of me to keep me warm, listening to the sound of a trickling mountain stream, only to open my eyes and see my step grandfather pissing into his bucket inches from my face.

Other days I would wander down to Black Rock, about a mile down the beach towards Newhaven. This was a part of the beach that was, unsurprisingly, full of black rocks with hundreds of small pools when the tide was out. I would sit on the rocks watching the crabs scuttle about, trying to build up the courage to pick one up. I was usually too scared, but I would however, tentatively pick up the dead ones and sit examining the shells and claws, marvelling at the alienness of the creatures.

My favourite pastime was to go to the beach on the stormiest of days, strip to my pants and run to the waters edge to be hit by a giant wave. I would curl into a ball and see how far I would be flung up the pebbly beach. On a good day I would make it all the way to the wall of the promenade. When the cold and bruises became a nuisance I would get dressed and squelch my way back to my grandmother's flat where, if she was back from work, I would be gently scolded and given some cocoa and crisps then I'd curl up with a book in front of the telly. If she wasn't back I would quickly hide the piss-pot in readiness for that night's entertainment, 'accidentally' nudge the old man awake, then go and sit by the window watching the rain lashing down on the lamp lit streets as people scurried back to the warmth of their loved ones.

This life ended when my father sent me a letter saying how he wanted me to come back and live with him. He told me he'd get me a motorbike. I was off like a shot.

Chapter 3

I spent about a year living with my father and his new family. One night my father woke me up and told me we had to leave immediately. We piled into the old campervan and fled the city. We'd gone about three miles when the van broke down. There was a lot of swearing. My stepmother took my stepsister and I to a nearby motel while my father waited for assistance. I'd never been in a motel and thought this was great. I felt like we were millionaires. The room had a colour telly and everything. My stepmother allowed me to stay up even later that night to watch a horror film with her while we waited for my father to get back with the campervan. He eventually returned with black hands and a vile tongue and sent me straight to bed.

The next morning we had breakfast in the restaurant. I loved the tiny boxes of cereal. There were loads to choose from. I felt like royalty. After eating we loaded up the campervan and drove for about two hours till we came upon a dirt track that went on for about a mile, seemingly leading nowhere. We were surrounded by woodland and eventually came to a clearing where there were half a dozen stables. Beyond these was huge old farmhouse covered in ivy. It had seen better days. My father got out of the van and went to the front door. I watched as he spent about twenty minutes talking with the man who apparently owned the place. At the end of the discussion I watched as my father fished a fistful of pound notes out of his pocket and gave them to the man. He returned to the van.

"We've got to wait here for a bit," he said. He had his serious face on so I didn't question him and neither did anybody else. A few minutes later the man came out carrying a duffel bag over his shoulder. He went to an old battered truck and drove off.

"Right kids," said my father cheerfully. "Out you get. We're on holiday."

We stayed at the old farmhouse for about two weeks. My father would disappear a couple of times a day for an hour or so and return with a very miserable look on his face, sometimes bringing with him a bag of chips for us all to share as the food and facilities in the farm left a lot to be desired. While we were there he gave me a magnificent pair of brown leather riding boots. I was quite excited as I'd never ridden a horse before but it turned out that the stables were empty. I never did figure out why he gave me those boots.

I spent most of the days there wandering through the woods looking for wildlife, climbing trees and deliberately trying to get myself lost just for the fun of it. There wasn't any electricity in the farmhouse so we all settled down quite early in the evenings. I read my books and we chatted by candlelight. There were surprisingly few fights. Eventually it was time to leave and I climbed into the van feeling sorry to be leaving the place.

We had travelled for a couple more hours when I could smell the sea. I looked out of the window and spotted a sign telling us that we were entering Brighton. I was overjoyed. I thanked my father profusely and asked him if we were going to stay with my maternal grandmother.

"No," he said. "We bloody aren't." I wasn't too bothered by this. It was one place in the world that I felt was my spiritual home and nothing could dampen my enthusiasm to be there.

We found a hotel by the sea front, unloaded the van and checked in. I couldn't believe my luck. Another hotel! But this wasn't like the motel, oh no, this was a real hotel with coffee machines and everything. It was a palace. While we were there my father would often go off with an Arabic looking man for hours at a time. He would return without telling us what he had been doing. His new friend seemed to be well-heeled and extremely charming and kind to us. My father told me that he used to be Mohammed Ali's bodyguard. I was awestruck.

After a week or so of being there I asked my father if I could go and visit my grandmother. He refused. I couldn't go anywhere. I longed go to the beach. From our hotel room, if you leant out of the window and looked right you could just see the sea beyond the Pavilion. When I didn't have my head 'stuck in a bloody book' as my father put it, I would often lean out of the window and gaze longingly at the sea.

My step-mother would often take me and my step-sister out to lunch at a nearby café where I would have a roast dinner followed by apple crumble and custard. I loved going there because we were always served by an old man with a hunchback. I'd never seen a real hunchback before. One day while we were eating I asked if I could go to the library on my own. I was allowed. My mother had always stipulated with whoever was looking after me that I must always be allowed access to the local libraries. My father and his mother always complained about this saying I was being antisocial and it wasn't healthy; I should be out playing with friends. They always gave in though. It shut me up. The library was ancient with a huge dinosaur skeleton in one of the rooms. I would always stop by and marvel at this on the way to the books. On this particular day I left the library to head back to the hotel when I had an idea. I would go and visit my grandmother. I took the route that led me through an old graveyard. It was full of stone tombs that stood about four feet high. Many were cracked and falling apart. I spent about an hour walking around reading the epitaphs. I looked through all of the cracked tombs trying to see if I could spot any skeletons.

"Could you spare me a few pence for a cup of tea?" I looked up to see and old bearded man in filthy clothes bearing down on me.

"I'm sorry, I've only got a fifty pence piece on me," I said nervously.

"There's a shop around the corner," he said. "I'll walk you to it to get some change."

"Erm, OK," I replied. We walked through the graveyard in the direction of the shop. He was very slow and asked if he could hold onto my arm to keep his balance. He stunk of booze and his hands were grubby but I let him.

"Why aren't you at school then?" he asked me. For some absurd reason it hadn't occurred to me that I hadn't actually been to school for about a month.

"I'm on holiday," I replied. We passed a group of young men with cans of beer in their hands. They looked at the old man scornfully and screwed their noses up at him.

"You want to tell your granddad to get a fucking bath," one of them said to me.

I blushed.

"He's not my granddad," I said.

They directed their attention to the old man.

"Leave the kid alone then, to dirty old pervert!" the young man shouted.

"It's alright, honestly," I butted in. "I'm just giving him a hand to get home."

The young man scoffed and skipped off to catch up with his mates.

"No bloody respect, some people," said the old man.

"I fought in the war, you know."

"Did you kill any Nazis?" I asked, intrigued.

"Hundreds," he replied.

"Wow."

"Where do you live then?" he asked me.

"All over the place," I said.

"Me too," he sighed.

"Haven't you got a home?"

"If it gets too cold I might spend the odd night in the Sally Army," he said. "Otherwise, I usually just get my head down under the West pier."

"I'd love that," I said, impressed. He took a bottle wrapped in a brown paper bag out of his coat pocket and took a swig. He offered me the bottle. I thought it would be rude to refuse so I took a small sip and nearly choked. He patted me on the back.

"Put hairs on your chest, that will," he said, chuckling. We reached the shop and I walked in while the old man waited outside. I approached the counter.

"Could you change a fifty pence piece please?" I asked the shopkeeper.

"If you're not going to buy anything, get out," he replied. I walked out of the shop and told the old man. He took the coin out of my hand and went into the shop. A minute later he came out with a can of cider.

"Here you go," he handed me the change. There was only fifteen pence left but I took it without complaining. He thanked me for my kindness and we parted company. It was getting late and I didn't want to get into trouble so I decided to postpone the visit to my grandmother and headed back to the hotel. It had started raining by the time I got there and I wondered if the old man would be able to find somewhere dry and warm to spend the night.

"Could I invite a friend to stay here tonight," I asked my father. "It's raining and I'm worried he might get pneumonia."

"What friend?" my dad asked. I told him about my encounter, adding that I might be able to find him under the pier.

"What have I bloody told you about talking to strangers?" he asked. "I'm not having a bloody tramp coming here." He sighed. "There's something wrong with you."

I took that as a 'no'.

A few days later I had finished my book and was allowed to go to the library again on my own. I decide to try my grandmother again. As I walked through the graveyard I spotted the old man sitting on a bench and gave him a wave. I didn't have any money on me so I didn't go over to him. He might be disappointed. He smiled and waved back at me. This attracted a strange look from a woman who passed me walking her dog. I looked at her quizzically. She started to say something to me but noticed her dog squatting in the path having a shit. She shook her head at me and bent down to pick up the turd with her hand inside a carrier bag. I continued on my way.

When I arrived at my grandmother's flat I knocked on the door. There was no answer. I prised open the bedroom window and climbed in. As I walked into the living room I noticed my step-grandfather sitting in his armchair with the piss-pot by his side.

"Who's there?" he asked. I ignored him and went to the kitchen to get a biscuit and a glass of squash. "I don't want any trouble. Just get out now and I won't call the police!" he shouted.

I walked into the living room and saw that he had

picked his white walking stick up and was brandishing it defensively. I turned on the television and sat on the sofa with my snack. I burped loudly.

"I'm blind," he whimpered. "Please, just go away. There's nothing of any value here." He was shaking now. I flicked through the channels on the television and, seeing there was nothing of any interest on, turned it off and returned my glass to the kitchen. On my way out of the flat I picked up his pot and hid it behind the sofa.

A few days later I returned to the flat and my Grandmother was in. She was shocked to see me but invited me in and gave me a drink and some crisps.

"Look who's here Sid," she said.

My step-grandfather was dressed in the same clothes and looked as if he hadn't moved since my last visit.

"I can't see who it is, I'm blind you stupid old cow!"

"Oh, take no notice of him," she said to me and beckoned me to sit down. "What are you doing in Brighton?" she asked. I told her the story. "Your mum's worried about you. She knows you're staying with your dad but she hasn't heard from you in weeks. What's your dad brought you down here for?"

"Don't really know," I replied. I didn't.

"You didn't come here the other day, did you?" she asked.

"No," I lied.

"Lying little bastard," said the old man.

"Shut up Sid," said my grandmother.

He muttered something under his breath and put his handkerchief under his glasses. He was soon asleep with his bottom set hanging out of his mouth as usual. After a bit of a chat I said goodbye and made my way back to the hotel.

A few days later my father went out one morning and

didn't come back. Days went by without seeing him. I asked my step-mother where he was and she said that he'd gone away with work for a while. She seemed quite upset and wouldn't tell me any more. About a week after my father's disappearance we packed up and got on the train back 'home'. My mother was there to meet us at the train station and took me back home with her.

I lived with my mother and my brother and about ten other people in a hippy commune. It was a big house full of people who smoked a lot and didn't eat meat. They were all very friendly but appeared to be half asleep most of the time. They seemed to have a very carefree approach to life. All problems were solved with a shrug of the shoulders and a sigh. They were however, very passionate about watering the multitude of strange smelling plants that filled the house and all hell would break loose if anybody let one of the plants die.

There was a couple who lived in the house - well I think they were a couple but wasn't totally sure because I had seen him kiss somebody else once – who had a massive pet rabbit that bit anybody who came near it. It was a nasty, horrible thing but they both doted on it. It did not live in a hutch but roamed the house chewing carpets and wires and shitting everywhere. One day the couple were having a blazing row in the kitchen. It had something to do with the plants and was getting more aggressive by the second. I decided to wait a while for my glass of squash and sat down on a beanbag watching them out of the corner of my eye. Suddenly the woman picked up a huge iron frying-pan and slung it across the kitchen at her partner. He dodged it with aplomb and I saw them both follow its trajectory as it flew on to decapitate the rabbit that had been minding its own business chewing the cupboard door. The relationship disintegrated after that but I was glad to see the back of the rabbit. There was just the pet albino rat left to contend with but he died of cancer about a week later and was buried under the cherry tree next to the rabbit. I've not been a fan of cherries ever since.

      I don't really remember much else happening during my time in the hippy commune but I think that's mainly because nothing actually did happen. My mother returned to college after a few months and it was time for me to move on.

Chapter 4

I spent some time living with my paternal grandparents. They lived in a small inner city two-up two-down and subsequently I had to share a bed with my uncle who tended to fart quite a lot. It was a tiny room and I would lie in bed intimidated by the images of Marc Bolan, Alvin Stardust and Gary Glitter who would stare down at me from the walls. It wasn't as pleasant as the bunk beds I used to share with my brother at my mother's flat, but I couldn't complain. We didn't talk much in the bed; we would mostly blow raspberries and kick each other until my grandmother came in and threatened to send my grandfather and his belt in. That usually shut us up.

I couldn't get enough of my grandmother's food. I'd never really had routine mealtimes with proper cooked dinners before. My grandmother would often make fun of my grandfather behind his back as she was in the kitchen preparing his favourite meal. If he were to ask her for a cup of tea from his armchair in the living room she would always secretly stick her fingers up at him before dutifully obeying his command.

My uncle Philip was nine years older than me, in his late teens at the time that I was living with them, and was great fun to be with. We would often all play cards for matchsticks, listening to military bands playing on the record player. He would often peek over my shoulder to see what cards I held. He had a collection of toy cars that we often played with when we weren't dressed as cowboys shooting each other with water pistols.

They had an old dog of an indeterminate breed that Philip doted on. I often walked the dog with him down to local park where we would throw sticks that the dog could never be bothered to retrieve. It was on one of these days when we were sitting by the brook that ran through the park that we were approached by three boys who were about the same age as me. They had an air of menace about them.

"Hey, look at that," one of them shouted, pointing at Philip. "A mongol and a mongrel!" His friends fell about laughing. I didn't know exactly what he meant but I knew it wasn't nice. I jumped up and threw my stick at him. He burst into tears as it hit his mouth and drew blood. They ran off shouting that they were going to get the police. Philip patted me on the back and we headed back home. We didn't go back to that park again.

About a month after the incident the dog died. Philip was inconsolable. For days he locked himself in his room and cried. I had to sleep on the sofa. It had wooden arms that hurt my head. I asked my grandmother if I could steal one of the many dogs that roamed the streets and give that to Philip to cheer him up but she said it could be dangerous. Instead I made him come down to one of the other parks in the area where I asked passers-by if they would let him pet their dogs. That seemed to do the trick so we made a habit out of it and within days I was back in a real bed again.

It wasn't until I actually went to live with my grandparents that I noticed that there was something different about Philip.

"Is Philip handicapped?" I asked my grandmother as we were walking to the shops one day.

"Pick your feet up. You'll wear those soles out," she said. I assumed she hadn't heard me and was about to repeat the question when I noticed that her eyes were shining. It was the only time in my life I saw this tough, funny woman cry. It turned out that although she suspected something, it wasn't actually confirmed by a doctor until he was two years old. Not that this affected their decision to lovingly raise him themselves, it was just unfortunate that they had to wait so long wondering what the problem was. I believe that the overprotective nature of my grandparents towards my uncle may have been a factor in my father going slightly off the rails. Having to focus so much time and energy on my uncle led them to pretty much let my father do what he wanted.

I remember walking back from school one day when an awful smell accosted my nostrils. I was about a mile away from the house at the time, in a heavily built-up part of the town. As I continued walking towards the house the smell grew stronger and stronger. People in the street were gagging, children were crying, so foetid was the stench. I got to the house and knocked on the door with the top of my jumper covering my nose. My grandmother answered the door.

"Quick, let me in," I said. "There's a horrible smell outside."

"That'll be the pig muck I've put in the garden," she said. "We've been to a farm today."

"I told her not to buy the stuff," my grandfather said, his head stuck in the paper. "She never bloody listens to a word I say." My grandmother stuck her customary two fingers up at him. He couldn't see her from where he was sitting but she still found it funny.

I walked into the kitchen and screamed. Staring at me from the kitchen sink was a pig's head. When my grandmother reassured me that it wasn't alive she went on to describe all of the wonderful meals she could make out of the head. I was aghast. Philip nearly choked on his beef dripping sandwich when he saw my face.

"We also got some chitterlings from the farm," she

said. "We'll have those for tea tonight."

"What are chitterlings?" I asked.

She pointed to a revolting looking pink mound on the table-top.

"Pig's intestines," she said. "Full of goodness. It'll put hairs on your chest." The smell emanating from the chitterlings was worse than the pig shit.

"Can I have chips instead?" I asked.

"Alright," she said. "You fussy little bugger."

I nearly collapsed with the relief.

The only time I ever remember being told off by them was when my grandfather spotted a horse chestnut tree sprouting in the garden.

"Where the bloody hell's that come from?" he asked my grandmother.

"I planted some conkers," I replied.

"What did you think you were playing at?" he asked me. "The bloody roots on those things go for miles. It'll destroy the foundations of all of the houses."

"Yeah, but at least we'll get some good conkers out of it," I said.

My grandmother's mother lived around the corner with my great aunt. As my aunt worked full-time, the duty of cleaning the house fell to my grandmother. I sometimes went with her. My great-grandmother was considerably senile. My grandmother had no shuck with this. I remember walking in the house one day.

"Morning mother," my grandmother said.

"Who are you?" said the old woman from her armchair by the fire.

"I'm your daughter. I've come to put the vac round."

"Get out of my house. You're not my daughter. Get out or I'll call the police!" She continued ranting, getting more and more agitated. My grandmother sighed and took a large white sheet from her bag. She unfolded it and with a well-practiced sweep, draped it over my great-grandmother's head until all you could see were her feet. This had the amazing effect of shutting her up.

"That's clever," I said to her my grandmother.

"It worked when I used to do it to the budgie," she replied. "It works with her too."

We spent the next hour or so dusting and cleaning the house. When we finished my grandmother made herself a cup of tea and poured me a glass of dandelion and burdock. We went into the living room to drink it while listening to the radio. My great-grandmother remained silent under her shroud. We got up to leave a while later and my grandmother removed the sheet from the old woman and put it back in her bag.

"Who are you? What do you want?" she said. "Get out before I call the police!"

"We're off now mother," said my grandmother. "See you tomorrow." We left.

Awful food aside, I was still quite sad when I had to move on from my grandparents. I'd grown really fond of Philip (farting in bed aside) and for the first time in my life there was physical pain in my chest as I waved goodbye to them all. Still, boarding school sounded great and it quickly took my mind off my loss.

Chapter 5

I'd been duped.

I'd liked to have thought that if my family had been aware that a former pupil had murdered a small girl they might have thought twice about sending me to boarding school. That if they'd have been aware that many of the teachers were either sadists or child molesters and that many of the kids were even worse… well, spilt milk and all that.

They were all there to wave me off: parents, grandparents, uncles, half-siblings, step-siblings. I felt like Dorothy going back to Kansas. I was bewildered by the reactions of most of the other boys, all crying, some loudly, some on their knees pleading with parents (oblivious to the violent repercussions that would ensue further down the line by the older boys). Wimps. As I smiled and waved through the coach window I noticed that my family (apart from Philip), although reciprocating my gestures, wouldn't actually meet my gaze. Ah well. I thought nothing more of it and looked around. Jesus, what was wrong with these kids. They were hysterical.

"Hey," I said to the boy next to me whose chest was heaving as he licked the twin streams of snot from his top lip. "What's wrong? You'll be seeing them again on Saturday."

When the subject of going to boarding school had first been raised by my mother, I had insisted on her giving me all of the details before I agreed to go. Not that I had a choice. As the snotty boy explained the reason for his tears, it dawned on me that my mother's explanation had been somewhat romanticised. It turned out that we weren't going home again until half-term. It would not be a pleasure filled holiday of midnight feasts and days lying in the sun watching the clouds. The realisation that I had been thrown to the wolves and would have to fend for myself for the next five years slowly dawned on me. As I felt my eyes begin to well with tears of fear and betrayal I realised that the other kids weren't so pathetic after all.

An hour and a half later the coach turned into the school gates. Although the school was set at the top of a hill with beautiful views all around, I was filled with a deep sense of foreboding. The big sign at the gate with the school name on may as well have read 'Work is Freedom'. As we got off the coach we were greeted by a thin weasley looking man wearing a gown and mortar board cap, completing the ensemble with a nasty looking piece of bamboo in his hand.

"Everybody stand on that line," he roared, pointing to a crudely drawn chalked line on the road, "and face this way!" He marched straight to me. "That includes you, you dithering idiot!" he sprayed in my face.

I don't think I'm going to like it here, I thought.

We were led through the school grounds towards the assembly hall. All of the buildings were spread out over acres of land and were made of dark wood resembling log cabins. There were three big fields with a forest at the bottom of one of them. I wanted to run and lose myself in its heart, escape this ghastly place and live off berries and river water. But I wasn't sure which ones were edible so I continued with the others. We passed the open air swimming pool and I was impressed by the beauty of the grounds, unaware of the downside of the structures we were passing. I would soon realise that the dormitories held no warmth in the winter and that the swimming pool was not heated. We entered the assembly hall. There was a tall fearsome looking grey man standing on a dais at the far end of the hall surrounded by a dozen or so teachers. All of them wore black gowns. I felt like a lame rabbit being hungrily surveyed by a murder of crows.

We were instructed to leave our suitcases by the door and stand facing the teachers. I could hear the other boys murmuring anxiously in the hall.

"Quiet!" yelled the Head. Silence and spirit fell simultaneously. "You!" he pointed his cane at a boy in the front row. "Name?"

"Rob," replied the boy.

The Headmasters lip curled. "Right. Let's make things clear shall we? ALWAYS show respect for the staff by calling them Sir; or Miss in Miss Hill's case," he nodded towards the birdlike figure standing to his left. "Also, boys are to be referred to and known by their surname only. Forget either of these rules and believe me, you will only forget once. So let's try again shall we?" he addressed the boy again.

"Gibson sir," he replied.

"Gibson, when we have finished here you will go directly to see the barber, whose premises you will find above the gym hall. As will you, you and you," he pointed to three other boys, me included.

"Are you a girl or one of those dirty hippies?" he pointed at me. I felt like a lump of ice had been dropped into my stomach and it was as if I couldn't lock my knees and I was going to fall. There was sniggering in the crowd.

"Neither, sir."

"Come here."

On unsteady legs I made my way to the front of the hall. All eyes were upon me. As soon as I was within arms reach the headmaster grabbed me by the hair and turned me to face the crowd. As an eleven year old there were three problems with my hair. Firstly it was in the process of turning from blond to brown and, unfortunately for me at the time, it was in its ginger phase. Secondly it was extremely thick and bushy. Thirdly it was long. My mother was a hippy, enough said. To my chagrin none of these characteristics had escaped the headmaster's beady eye. My head hurt and I fought back the tears.

"There's no excuse for this!" he roared. "This is not Cheltenham Ladies College; it is a boarding school for boys." He turned to the birdlike teacher. "Miss Hill, would you be so kind as to loan me your ribbon?" He pulled my hair tight and put the ribbon around it. "You will not remove that ribbon until you have had your head shaved. If you do I will make sure you regret it."

At that age I was smart enough to make what proved to be a very wise decision. I didn't know the man, I didn't respect his opinion, therefore I wasn't offended by it, and I also knew that to do as I was told would result in indescribable suffering at the hands of my fellow pupils for the next five years. If I was to claw back any credibility from my peers I only had one option. I only wanted to be left alone. I was not a bad person, so it was with a heavy heart and no small amount of terror that I raised my hand to my head, pulled out the ribbon and threw it on the floor. It landed on the headmaster's shoes.

"No," I said.

I looked up. The crowd roared. I had not only redeemed myself, I was a hero. I smiled. I did not even feel the blow to my temple that rendered me unconscious and confined me to the Sick Bay for the night.

And that was day one.

Chapter 6

I awoke the next morning from a wonderful dream in which I was eating cockles on Brighton beach, watching children skim pebbles across the sea. I rubbed my eyes and took in my surroundings. The Sick Bay was a large brightly lit room that had about twenty beds in it, only two of which were occupied. The other bed contained a boy with a blue head and a black eye. He was staring at me.

"Nits?" I asked.

"No," he replied, and turned away. We didn't speak again.

My head was throbbing and I was feeling more than a little sorry for myself.

The matron entered the room. She was stereotypically middle-aged with an eye-catching chest and a stern disposition. It turned out she was multi-talented. As well as manning the sick bay single handed she was also the school seamstress. Her most infamous duty however, was the creation of the jam that was on all of the dining tables. It was a sloppy mess with a rather pungent aroma. As her name was Polly this concoction was affectionately known to the boys as 'Polly's Period' and was often used as a dare in the dining hall. She told us to get dressed immediately then make our way to the dining hall for breakfast.

"Where is it?" I asked.

"Use your initiative," she replied.

As we entered the dining hall I looked around. There were about fifty square tables, each seating eight people. There was rectangular table in the middle of the hall where the teacher sat. It was from this table that a deep voice immediately roared at us.

"You two are ten minutes late. See me after

breakfast!"

"But we've been…" I began.

"Don't argue. Go and sit down at that table." He indicated a table in the corner with two empty seats. We went and sat down.

"Did I tell you to sit?" asked one of two very big boys who were sitting together at the table. I was to find out very quickly that these were the Table Heads. Each table had six younger boys and two fifth years who oversaw the proceedings at the table.

"No," I replied.

"You call me "Sir", understand?"

"No sir,"

"That's better. Now sit down and put your hand out, palm down." I reluctantly did as I was told. I saw the other boys at the table wincing. That didn't bode well. The table head then picked up the ceramic salt pot and sprinkled salt on the back of my hand. He then brought the salt pot down hard, ground the pot deep onto my hand and dragged it down over my fingers, tearing the skin and drawing blood. I fought back the urge to scream but couldn't stop the tears that silently rolled down my cheeks.

"Oy, Nit-boy; your turn. Hand out." I turned and saw the colour drain from the boy's face as he put out his extremely shaky hand. As the sound of his scream filled the room everybody dropped their cutlery and looked across at our table. A huge cheer rose from all of the tables.

The teacher banged his mug on the table to quieten us all. Silence fell.

"For what we are about to receive, may the Lord make us truly thankful," he said with his head down.

"Amen," everybody said.

"Now keep the noise down and get on with your

breakfast!" he bellowed, ignoring the sobs coming from nit-boy.

"Now you know what happens when you break the rules of the table," said the other table head.

"What are the rules?" I asked, and then quickly added "sir."

"You'll find out as we go along," he replied. By the end of that meal I found out, courtesy of one of the other boys that putting your elbows on the table was another mistake not to be made.

Fifteen minutes after we had started breakfast the teacher banged on his table to attract our attention.

"Listen in!" he called. "For the benefit of our late arrivals, inspection will be at 8.30 sharp every morning apart from Sunday when it will be 9 O'clock. You are to have your beds made with hospital corners; your bedside cupboard will be tidy and your bed space spotless. As this morning is Tuesday you will put out your laundry. You will lay the following items on a towel on your bed ready for inspection: two pairs of pants, two pairs of socks and two shirts, all with the nametags showing, ready to be rolled up and put in the laundry basket. Now finish your breakfast and get back to your dormitories."

"How can we have all of those dirty clothes already?" one of the boys at the table asked. "We've only been here for a day."

"I'd just do it without asking questions, if I were you," replied the table head.

When I had returned to the dormitory I was shown my bed by the house captain and set about preparing for the inspection when I heard a commotion from the other end of the dorm. I walked down and saw one of the boys crying and being held back from his bed space by two of the other boys. I could see why he was crying. Somebody had taken his pants from his neatly presented laundry roll and had pinned them to his head board with a big skid mark showing. As it stood he had already been christened 'Odd Bod' by the other boys after a character from a Carry-on film, due to his unfeasibly large head. It seemed that already people were being assigned nicknames; I'd heard about half a dozen so far. These were to define us for the next five years. The boys responsible told Odd Bod that they would kill him if he tried to take them down before inspection. He reluctantly complied. A few minutes later the boy who had been appointed house-captain shouted for us all to stand by our beds as the housemaster was on his way to inspect us.

    He walked in holding a slipper. Oh God, I thought. He approached the first bed and stood scrutinising the boy's uniform and bed space. He kicked the side of the boy's bed.

    "What the hell do you call those?" he asked, indicating the folded corners of the blanket.

    "Hospital corners, sir," the boy replied.

    "Those are hospital corners," the housemaster shouted, pointing to the bed of the house captain. "These are a bloody shambles. Bend over!"

    The boy bent over the end of his bed, proffering his backside to the man. Whack! The slipper came down hard.

    "Now sort it out. Now you can all listen to this," he shouted. "For every single problem I find at inspection, the boy responsible will be slippered. The number of things I find wrong will correspond with the number of times you are punished. Are we all clear on that?"

    There was a murmured acquiescence from the dorm. I glanced down at my own hospital corners. They weren't very good. My insides turned to ice as I watched him steadily make his way towards my bed. Two other boys had been slippered so far. He stood so close I could smell the sugar puffs on his breath, his nose about an inch from mine as he stooped over me.

"Pick up your shoes," he whispered. I looked down. I thought my shoes were alright. It was the hospital corners I was worried about.

"They're disgusting," he said as he smeared his greasy finger across the highly polished black leather. "There is nothing on this earth worse than filthy shoes. They are a disgrace, what are they?" he asked.

"A disgrace, sir," I replied. If he honestly thought there was nothing worse than shoes that weren't polished properly, well, I could show him a few things. Still, best keep my trap shut, I thought.

He looked up and surveyed his audience.

"If anyone here thinks ..." he stopped as he caught sight of the pants. His eyes bulged and his face grew scarlet. He marched down to the boy's bed. I rejoiced in the knowledge that he had forgotten all about me.

"Who did this?" he whispered coldly to the boy. "It obviously wasn't you, so who was it?"

"It *was* me sir," the boy replied.

The housemaster sighed. "Very well, bend over." He then proceeded to administer one particularly lacklustre attempt at a slippering. "If I catch any of you doing practical jokes like this ever again, I will make sure that joking will be the last thing on your mind for quite some time," he shouted, then stormed out of the dorm without even inspecting the last two beds.

Throughout the day whichever class we were to attend we were issued with our exercise books and told that we must put a cover on each of them by the next lesson. Some boys were prepared for this and had brought fancy sheets of wallpaper with them to decorate them with; by doing so they had displayed their colours and therefore had to pay the price. Just like the one boy who stated that he had pen-pals in thirty-six different countries. I just used brown paper on my books and as far as any hobbies that I had went, well, I realised pretty quickly that I had better keep them to myself.

We were informed that prep (supervised homework) would take place between 7pm and 8.30pm every night except Friday and Saturday. Detention, for those concerned, was from 3.30pm until 4.30pm weekdays and 2pm until 3pm on weekends. We were told a multitude of other rules and regulations but my head was still in a whirl and my insides like jelly. I had still not adapted to this new life and nobody was attempting to ease me into it gently. I desperately wanted to go home. We were told that every week we must write a letter to our parents informing them of our progress. I decided to write and tell my mum that this just wasn't working and she'd better come and get me and send me to a normal school where I could go home every day and the teachers weren't monsters. It was decided. I was sure she'd take my comments on board and comply with my request once I'd told her what it was really like. That meant I only had to put up with the place for a couple of weeks at worst. This resolution helped me get through the first week. I now had hope.

That Sunday night I wrote my letter. I felt it was best not to be ambiguous. The letter went something like this:

'Dear mum,

Please come and get me. It's horrible. The teachers are horrible and the other boys are horrible. I hate it. Please

please please come and take me home.' That should do it, I thought.

I spent the rest of the next two weeks sprinting back to the dormitory after breakfast to see if the housemaster had a letter for me. I imagined my mother opening my letter and being horrified by my revelations and rushing to rescue me. Of course this didn't happen. She told me that it was perfectly natural to be homesick and I would soon get over it. I then wrote to both sets of grandparents and my father begging them all to rescue me but their sentiments mirrored those of my mother. They just didn't understand that there was more to it than just plain old homesickness. The place just felt wrong.

One night as I walked back from the ablution block I heard a low humming noise. I looked up into the clear night sky and watched a distant tiny light traverse across the sky and disappear over the horizon. I imagined being on the aeroplane with my family, on the way to some exotic sandy location sitting at the window looking down at the lights below before crossing the ocean; listening to the roar of the engine while everyone else dozed in the reclined chairs.

"Get a bloody move on, boy," shouted the housemaster from the dormitory door. I looked down and obediently walked back to my bed.

Chapter 7

The months crawled past and I felt I had adapted well and had the place pretty much sussed out. I would occasionally have flashbacks to my early days at the school and I would cringe at my naivety. What a child I had been! I had grown. I could handle anything.

One night I was reading a book with my torch under the blanket when I heard voices from a bed nearby.

"Put it in your mouth," a voice whispered. I recognised it as one of the older boys from further down the dorm.

"I don't want to," stressed the younger boy.

"Go on you puff, just do it!" urged the older boy. That's rich, I thought.

"No, leave me alone."

"You'd better watch your back, you little shithouse." Silence. About a minute later there was a gentle tap on my shoulder. I nearly wet myself with fright.

"Can I borrow your torch?" It was one of the other kids who had obviously been totally oblivious to what I had just listened to.

"Jesus Christ!" I exclaimed, breathing a huge sigh of relief. "Piss off, I'm using it."

"Suit yourself, Stonekicker," he muttered and went back to his bed.

Due to the fact that I had not really gelled with anybody, I was known as 'Stonekicker,' somebody without friends who just stands in the schoolyard with his head down, hands in pockets, aimlessly kicking stones. I wasn't particularly bothered by this name.

I woke at about 2am, shocked out of my sleep by a fart as loud as a gunshot. I looked around. Nobody else seemed to have been disturbed by it. It wasn't fair that I should be the only one to suffer an interrupted sleep. I got out of bed and tiptoed over to the bedwetter. I gently shook him awake.

"What do you want?" he asked.

"Sorry to bother you at this time of night; I just wanted to ask you something," I said.

"What?"

"Have you pissed yet?"

"Fuck off and leave me alone."

"Ok. Sorry about that." I got back into bed, pleased in the knowledge that I wasn't the only one struggling to get to sleep anymore; and feeling just a tiny bit guilty about upsetting the boy universally known as 'Slash'.

The next night I was woken up by the sound of two kids giggling. I watched as they gathered clothes in a pile and began stuffing them inside their beds.

"What are you doing?" I asked

"Making it look like we're in bed for when the housemaster comes patrolling," one of them replied. I couldn't remember his real name. Everyone called him Luke due to his slender frame, pale skin and fine blond hair. Apparently people thought that he looked like he had leukaemia, hence the nickname Luke.

"Where are going then?" I asked.

"Out," he replied mysteriously. "Do you want to come?"

"Ok," I replied excitedly. I followed suit and stuffed my bed with clothes and shaped them until they vaguely resembled the outline of a body.

"Bring your torch," said Luke. I put on my slippers and dressing gown and followed them as they crept silently out of the dormitory and into the night.

We stayed in the shadows, close to the buildings as we passed the other dormitories and headed into the Junior Games Room. This was where the first to third years were allowed to associate out of school hours. It contained a tuck shop, table-tennis tables and bright yellow plastic moulded tables and chairs by the windows. Adjacent to the JGR was the TV room. This was where we were going.

"What are we doing in here," I asked. Luke's companion was a boy who was short for his age, had blond hair and wore black national health glasses, known to everybody as Joe 90.

"The third years watched a dirty video in Science today. I thought we could watch it," he said.

"Cool."

I watched as they fumbled through the collection of education videos until they found the right one. Joe then turned on the TV and put the film into the huge clunking VCR.

"Oy, Stonekicker, stay by the window and keep a look out while we watch it."

I walked over to the window, checked that the coast was clear and drew the curtains closed. The TV screen lit up the whole room and I had to double check there were no cracks in the curtains. I looked at the screen. I couldn't believe my eyes; it was an educational video about childbirth.

"Phoar, look at the size of her tits!" cried Joe as he stared at the image of a young woman in the process of giving birth.

"We'll get to see her fanny in a minute," said Luke.

I couldn't believe they were getting turned on by something like this, but I did find it curiously fascinating. I'd only ever seen the odd photograph of a naked woman in the scraps of old porno mags that the boys sold to each other. This was a real live woman and I was transfixed until I noticed the curtains suddenly light up and I looked out of the window.

"Shit! Turn it off. Fat Dog's coming". This was how we lovingly referred to the deputy head, a tall man who was also very portly. Luke hit the switch and we all dived under the bench that ran along the wall opposite the TV. We heard the external door creak open and footsteps heading our way.

I held my breath. A large pair of moccasin shoes came into view. Joe's foot was digging into my shoulder. I watched as the feet headed towards the TV where they paused for a minute before turning around and heading back out of the door. I had little doubt that he knew somebody was in there. I guess he just couldn't be bothered with the hassle of having to do something about it. Whatever the case, the relief I felt was indescribable.

On the way back to the dormitory we dropped by the Headmasters study. After a couple of minutes working on the window latch we managed to get it open and we all crawled inside. We went inside and had a nose around. I was curious about the kind of books he might be interested in. There were books by Thomas Hughes, George MacDonald Frazer, Niccolo Machiavelli, a book called 'Philosophy in the bedroom' by someone called the Marquis de Sade, and a book called 'The Art of War' by Sun Tzu. I'd heard of Tom Brown's Schooldays but as far as the rest were concerned I didn't have a clue. I was rudely brought to my senses by a loud plopping sound. I turned and noticed the door to the Headmaster's en-suite toilet ajar, and there, sitting on the toilet with his pants around his ankles was Luke.

"What on earth are you playing at," I asked incredulously.

"Couldn't resist it," he replied while pulling up his pyjama bottoms. "I'd love to see his face when he comes in tomorrow."

"You haven't wiped your arse," said Joe.

"I want him to see it in its full glory," said Luke. "Bog-roll will only spoil the effect." I could see his point.

"Come on, Fat-dog's still on the prowl. We'd better get back," I said. All in all it had been a very enlightening and exciting night. I was still shaking with the comedown from the adrenalin rush as I crawled back into bed ten minutes later.

Chapter 8

One weekend in October I was sitting at the top of the football field reading when I felt a sudden sharp pain in the side of my head. This was followed by the sound of laughter. There was a group of three third years standing about twenty feet from me. One of them, Mossy as he was known, had a catapult in his hand. What I had been hit with was a small metal nut.

"Sorry about that mate," he shouted and walked over to me. "I honestly didn't think it would hit you."

I weighed up my options and realised that I'd better keep my mouth shut. "It's ok," I replied. "It did hurt though."

"Yeah. Did you see what happened to the nut?"

I picked it up off the grass.

"Here you go," I handed him the nut and looked at the catapult. It was magnificent. It was made of aluminium and had black tape wrapped around the handle to improve the grip. "Can I have a go?" I asked.

"You're not going to let him are you?" one of the other boys asked him.

"It's alright," the boy turned to his friends. "He's not a bad kid. I'll let him have a go." I couldn't see the expression on his face as he had his back turned to me, but his friends all nodded their heads in agreement. "Here you go," he offered me the catapult. "I'll show you how it's done. Are you right-handed?"

"Yes."

He put the catapult in my left hand.

"Put the nut in the rubber cup, squeeze tight and pull back with your right hand holding the catapult as tight as you can with your left. Look for what you want to hit and lift your left thumb until what you're aiming at looks like it's just resting on top of your thumb."

I did as I was told.

"Got that," I said.

"Fire."

I let go of the rubber cup and watched as my thumb nail exploded before my eyes. It took a couple of seconds for the pain to register, but when it did the pain was indescribable. All of the beatings I had ever experienced put together wouldn't have come close to the agony I felt. The gang of boys were howling with laughter as they retrieved the catapult and ran off towards the dormitories. I felt dizzy and sick. I collapsed onto the grass trying to grab my thumb tight to make the pain go away but I couldn't touch it. I looked at the mess and wondered if it would leave me deformed. The nail had split apart and my thumb was gushing blood as the swelling kicked in. I could feel every heartbeat through the tip. Once the worst of the sharp, stabbing pain had subsided and I was left with a dull throb I got to my feet and made my way towards Sick Bay. As I walked past the staff room the geography teacher spotted me and rushed over.

"What the hell have you been playing at?" he asked as he noticed my thumb.

"Nothing, sir." I suspected catapults would be a banned item and didn't want to make things worse. I also knew that telling on the others might not be such a good idea either.

"I'm not playing games here, son. You've got one last chance to tell me what happened," he said. He was getting angry now and I didn't need it. I just wanted my thumb to stop hurting. So I told him. Everything.

An hour later I was back in the dormitory having had

my thumb bandaged when Mossy and his cronies walked in.

"I've just had that fucking geography teacher confiscate my catapult and put me in detention next Saturday thanks to you, you grassing little bastard!" he shouted.

"I didn't have any choice," I answered. I was scared but I was also in pain and very angry.

"Of course you had a choice. You could have kept your fucking mouth shut." He advanced towards me. I looked around and grabbed the nearest thing to hand, a pencil.

"You come near me and I'll stab you in the eye." He grabbed the pencil out of my good hand, reached across and grabbed my bandaged thumb and squeezed. I nearly fainted and dropped to my knees.

"You'll give me all of your pocket money until Christmas to pay for a new catapult. Do you understand?"

"Yes," I whispered in agony.

"Louder."

"Yes," I shouted.

"That's better. Now if you cross me again you're dead. Do you hear me you dirty little grass?"

He walked out of the dormitory, leaving me sitting on the floor feeling more shame than pain. No one else would look at me. I had always prided myself in being able to see the funny side in absolutely anything. I was struggling here, that was for sure. Still, there was no way I was going to let him get away with humiliating me like that. I didn't care how big he was or how many mates he had. I just had to bide my time.

That night, it being Saturday, a few of the others invited me down to the canteen to play games or watch TV.

I knew it was out of sympathy and I could have done without that. I declined and spent the evening on my own in the dorm, reading and trying to figure out what I had to do to survive in this place.

The following Monday morning an opportunity for revenge fell into my lap. I'd lost a slipper and subsequently I was the last one in the dorm to get across to the ablution block after we'd all got out of bed. I looked at all of the unmade beds and was struck with a fantastic idea. The dormitory was empty as I walked up to Mossy's bed. I pulled back the blanket and top sheet and peed on his bed. I then found my slipper and swiftly went across to do my ablutions. I walked in, found an empty sink and spotted Mossy at the other end of the block. He hadn't noticed me come in last. I breathed a sigh of relief and waited with growing excitement for him to finish cleaning himself. He was one of the last ones to finish because he always had a shave in the morning. He had the occasional bit of bum-fluff on his chin but never enough to warrant a daily shave. I guessed it just made him feel that much more of a man than the rest of us. I left him there and returned to the dorm. The majority of boys were already back and would have been getting themselves ready for breakfast were it not for the commotion coming from Mossy's bed-space. He walked back into the dormitory and was greeted by a cacophony of sneers of disgust mingled with howls of derisory laughter.

"Here he is, the dirty bastard!" someone shouted

"Oy, Piss-bed, forget to put your nappy on last night?" shouted Stig.

"What are you going on ab…?" He spotted his bed and his face went scarlet. "That wasn't me," he blurted.

"Oh, did you have someone else in bed with you then,

you dirty bummer," said Stig. Even in his current state of fury Mossy knew better than to pick a fight with Stig. "So what is it, are you bent and shagging a piss-bed or did you do it yourself? I personally don't know which is worse."

"I didn't do it, I tell ya!" yelled Mossy. He then burst into tears and ran out of the dormitory.

"I think we should call him 'Nappy-rash' from now on," called Luke. Everybody laughed. The name stuck.

As I made my way to breakfast I realised that although the pain in my thumb was getting me down, my spirits were higher than they'd been in quite some time. Later that day the housemaster issued him with a plastic sheet which only compounded his misery. I didn't doubt for a minute that Nappy-rash - as he would be forever known - suspected me. His friends had immediately disassociated themselves from him following his 'indiscretion' and without them to back him up he was lost. He spent the rest of the term on his own, constantly being bombarded with abuse. I think the other boys attacked him so much more viciously than the other victims because of his previous reputation as a cool hard man. They found his fall from grace made him all the more pathetic.

He didn't return to the school after Christmas. Good riddance to bad rubbish, I thought.

Chapter 9

The whole school was in a state of exhilaration at the announcement that we were to have a Bonfire Night party on Saturday night. We were also informed that it would be managed with military precision by the deputy head. None of us (apart from the house captains) would be permitted to touch the fireworks as he was to orchestrate the display. Apparently there were going to be jacket potatoes as well. I loved jacket potatoes (as long as they had real butter in).

Joe and Luke thought it would be fun to go to the village prior to the party to get some bangers. I had nothing else to do, so I tagged along. After half an hour of begging we eventually got an adult to go into the shop for us to buy the bangers and we made our way back towards school. On the way we stopped by the river bank to have a crafty fag.

"What are you going to do with those bangers?" I asked them. "We're not allowed to buy fireworks."

"Wait and see," said Joe mysteriously.

Luke suddenly jumped to his feet. "Look, a toad!" he said. "I was hoping I'd find one here. Quick, grab it."

"I'm not touching it," I said. The thought of touching the slimy skin made me shudder.

"I'll get it," said Joe. He spent the next five minutes catching and losing the toad before he eventually had it in a secure grip in his hands.

"Turn it round so I can see its arse," said Luke. I watched in horror as Luke proceeded to stick one of the bangers in the toad's rectum. "Hold it still!" he urged Joe.

"I'm trying," he said. "It's not easy."

"Give me the matches," Luke said to me. I reluctantly handed them to him. I looked at the toad. It was squirming, trying to escape but Joe held on tight. It was quiet and its eyes were bulging but I thought that they were always like that anyway. Luke struck the match and lit the wick making Joe keep hold of the toad until the last second. We waited. "Run!" he shouted. Joe put the toad on the ground and we ran to a distance of about ten feet and watched as the toad was blown to smithereens.

As we walked back to the school, Luke and Joe were congratulating themselves on a job well done. I had mixed emotions. Although I really did feel sad for the poor toad, I had to admit that I had found the whole process of the toad's demise mesmerizing.

Chapter 10

As I was laying out my laundry for inspection one Tuesday I noticed a small skid-mark in one of my pairs of pants. I panicked. Without thinking I grabbed my toothbrush and ran to the ablution block to wet it. I returned and crouched down and scrubbed the mark until it disappeared. I then ran back to the ablution block and stuck the damp pants under the hand dryer. I had to spend all of my pocket money that week on a new toothbrush, but it was worth it. That kind of humiliation could be the death of you.

While waiting in the Science block hallway to go into Chemistry I noticed Slash leaning against the window with his head down. Curious, I went to see what he was doing.

"Hello Marcus," he said.

"What the hell do you think you're doing?" I asked.

"What?" he asked.

"Calling me by my first name, you idiot."

"What's wrong with that?" he seemed genuinely confused.

"Everyone will think we're puffs," I said. "Jesus Christ." I looked around for witnesses. "We're lucky. It looks like you've got away with it this time. Anyway," I said, "What are you doing?"

"Look," he said. He had a daddy long-legs in each hand. "See the bit that sticks out of that one's tail-like thing?"

"Yeah, what about it?" I asked.

"That's a male Daddy long-legs and the other one has a hole at the end of its tail which means it's a female."

"Fascinating," I turned to walk back.

"Hang on," he said. "Watch this. You can make them have sex."

"Go on then," I said and watched with morbid curiosity as he rammed the male's organ into the female's orifice and stuck them together. He then let go and they fell onto the window ledge in an enforced embrace where they writhed about a bit until one of them died. "Cool," I said and spent the next five minutes catching as many as I could and doing the same until we were called into class.

This kind of thing turned into a bit of a hobby. By watching Slash every day in the hallway I learnt a few ways to pass the time while waiting for classes; I learnt that if you managed to catch a fly, pull its wings off and stick a compass needle through it, it would spin around while impaled for ages before it died. Killing wasps by firing paper pellets from an elastic band was also great fun. The best trick by far though, was burning ants with a magnifying glass; you didn't even need to get your hands dirty for that one. I eventually gave up the hobby when people started to think that I had found a new friend in Slash.

That evening when I went to the canteen to buy a new toothbrush I was greeted by the English teacher whose turn it was to supervise.

"I've caught one of the boys entrusted to run the tuck shop with his hand in the till," he told me.

"Oh dear," I said.

"Yes, indeed. How do you feel about having the job?" he asked me.

I was honoured.

"I'd love to sir," I replied.

"Bear in mind you'll be on trial for the first two weeks. You can start this Saturday night."

"Thanks very much sir," I said.

That Saturday night after tea I went straight to the

canteen to start my new job. I was to be working side by side with Luke. It was heaven. There were chocolate, crisps, biscuits, cans of pop and hot dogs which we were allowed to cook. We were also given a float of two pounds to use for change. All I had to do was keep my hands to myself and I could keep this highly sought-after position. I was sacked the next day for thieving. Nobody seemed to be able to hold on to the position for more than a couple of weeks. I believed that if the school meals had been even barely edible I might have refrained from scoffing all of the hot dogs in the canteen. At least the other boys had had a bit of a reprieve from having their tuck stolen. Unfortunately for them it was short-lived.

Over the coming months I heard snippets of rumours filtering down from the years above regarding the former pupil who had killed a girl. By all accounts it was quite straightforward; he had gone home at the end of term and had thrown his little sister down the stairs, breaking her neck instantly. I could kind of empathise. There had been many occasions when my brother and I had hospitalised each other through horseplay. I lost count of the amount of times I had smashed his head through the glass panels of the door between the living room and dining room. I had once shot him at point-blank range with my dad's air pistol and the pellet had to be picked out of his back with tweezers. I had whipped him across the back with the plastic-coated wire that held up the net curtains; this had drawn a considerable amount of blood. Don't get me wrong, my brother was no angel. He once slit my throat with a kitchen knife and broke my finger by slamming a door on it deliberately. Our parents were never able to ascertain who the instigator was on any of the occasions, so adept were we at lying. In a futile attempt to avert any further violent incidents my father would just beat the hell out of the pair of us.

When my brother came to the boarding school I was in the fourth year. He struggled to settle in and would frequently come to me in a sorry state hoping that I would rescue him from whatever was upsetting him.

"Here's your baby brother crying like a girl again," the other boys would taunt. "Go and give him a cuddle!"

I would look at the sorry state my brother would be in and tell him to fuck off and leave me alone. This was what they all wanted. I maintained my kudos among my peers and lived to fight another day.

Amazingly my brother found an ally in the most unlikely of places. There was a fifth year who was a total thug and the toughest bully in the school. He was the table-head on my brother's table. It transpired that my grandmother had been his favourite dinner-lady at junior school. Because of this he took my brother under his wing. He would bully the other kids on the table into giving my brother the richest pickings at meal times and he insisted that my brother tell him if anybody was picking on him. I soon saw what happened to those boys that did make this mistake and it wasn't pretty. He even had stern words with me at one point, insisting that I take on a greater role in looking after my brother. Even though I was rated as being the sixth hardest boy in the fourth year I knew better than to cross this psychopath. Although my brother had his own Guardian Demon he still struggled to cope in the school and after what I guess was a pretty miserable year my mother decided to remove him and put him in a normal school. Well, I remember thinking, alright for some!

Chapter 11

Mr McEwan kept me back after English one day to speak to me.

"Did you know, I've seen something in you that sets you apart from the other boys," he said. He'd seemed to have forgotten my indiscretion in the tuck-shop. "You're a strapping young lad with excellent posture. Are you aware of that?"

"No sir," I said, wondering where the hell this was going.

"You may have noticed that I run the Army cadets behind the Art block on a Friday evening. You've got to have something pretty special about you to be a part of something like that, and I think you've got what it takes. What would you say about coming along this Friday and giving it a go?"

"Do I get to fire a gun sir?" I asked.

He laughed.

"Yes, eventually you'll get the opportunity to master the art of firing an S.L.R." I didn't know what S.L.R. stood for but I guessed it was a gun of some sort, hopefully like the ones the gunslingers used in the cowboy films.

"Yes I'd love to sir," I said, genuinely pleased that he thought I was good enough to join.

"Right, see you on Friday at six," he said." If you take to it we'll see if we can't sort you out with a uniform."

I turned up on time on the Friday night and something immediately struck me as odd. All of the other boys who were in the cadets, without exception, had something in common. It wasn't the fact that they were all dressed identically in combats, berets and shiny boots. It was something else. They were all wankers. And worst of all was the fact that the one who was in charge of the other boys, the Lance Corporal, was Huey. This was a boy who seemed to be failing miserably in the game of survival. He was one of the rich kids who were constantly losing their tuck to the other boys. It wasn't even done behind his back; boys would just spot him eating something and take it off him. All he would do to retaliate was cry. There was more than one occasion when it was me that had relieved him of his goodies. It was also me that had actually christened him the name Huey after he got travel sick once on the coach back to school. The nickname had stuck and it was all he had been known as for the last two years. Ah well, I thought, maybe he's not the type to hold a grudge. The English teacher came out from behind the Art block dressed in full army uniform with a pay stick under his arm. This was an item that resembled large compasses that army types liked to carry about their person looking all soldiery.

"Attention!" shouted Huey. Everybody bashed their heels together and stuck their noses in the air.

After quite a bit of marching around, wheeling left and right and the odd 'About turn' and a final 'Fall out' the teacher asked me if I had enjoyed the experience.

"Yes sir," I said. "When do I get to shoot a gun?"

"Soon, soon," he replied. "Now come with me and we'll sort you out with a uniform."

I followed him to the clothing store where he told me to remove my clothes and try on different items of clothing to find some that fit. We were eventually done and he sent me back to the dorm to put the uniform away neatly.

The following Friday we were standing at ease waiting for the teacher, or 'Sergeant Major' as he was known on a Friday.

"Attention!" squealed Huey. We all complied. He

marched straight up to me. "What the hell do you call those?" he asked, pointing at the bits of green cloth wrapped around my ankles.

"Er, Putties," I replied.

"Look at the state of them. Now you make sure they are put on in the same fashion as the other soldiers or I'll have you on Jankers!"

"Yes, Lance Corporal," I replied. I didn't have a clue what he was going on about but I thought I'd better humour him.

"All right, all right," came the voice of the English teacher." Give the lad a chance; he's still new to the game." Huey backed off. I silently mouthed the words 'you're fucking dead' to him and smiled. We spent the next hour doing more of the usual marching, stamping, saluting and twirling about without a gun in sight. I was becoming slightly disillusioned with this cadet malarkey.

The following Friday I finally got to learn what an S.L.R. was. It wasn't the shiny pistol I had been hoping for but it was alright. We weren't allowed bullets, or rounds as that type liked to call it, but I still took great pleasure in pointing it at Huey's face when the teacher wasn't looking. He visibly paled but knew better than to report me for it after I'd stuck his head down the toilet following last week's indiscretion.

After a month or two we eventually got round to being taken to a range to practice. As I had hoped I took to the art of firing a rifle marvellously. The teacher was so impressed he soon entered me into county competitions and I was considered one of the best marksmen the school had ever had. I loved the fact that the teacher thought so much of me; so much so that it was with a heavy heart that I had to tell him that I had to leave cadets. It unfortunately clashed with a brilliant show on TV that had a magic monkey that could do martial arts.

Chapter 12

One weekend the English teacher asked me if I'd like to choose a couple of friends to go? on a trip to the cinema with him. I couldn't believe my ears. Every single time he had [obscured] Still, I wasn't [obscured] me to [obscured] apades, but that [obscured] m or any other boys for that matter. I generally liked to keep myself to myself. I had to choose someone to come on the trip though, so I invited them along.

"Who's a little teacher's pet then," said Luke.

"Do you want to come or not?" I asked him.

"Yeah, course I do. I haven't been to the pictures in years."

"Well, stop giving me shit then," I said. "I'm not a teacher's pet. He just rewards kids that do well in English. I can't help it if you're too thick to throw shit at and he doesn't invite you."

"Oh, hark at Shakespeare here," he nodded to Joe. "You're not so smart yourself, you know. You've never got an A in any of the tests."

"He says I've got a lot of potential, so stick that up your arse," I was getting annoyed now. I wished I hadn't invited them.

We knocked on the door of his flat at about six o'clock. He'd told us we didn't have to wear uniform for the trip which was a real treat. Joe and Luke had their best clothes on and Luke stunk to high heaven of poor cologne. Unfortunately I only had one pair of old jeans and a sweat shirt that had seen better days but that didn't bother me. I was just glad to be getting out.

"Have you had a bloody bath in cheap aftershave?" I asked him.

The door opened. The teacher was dressed in his usual tweed suit and tie but he seemed to have overdone it on the aftershave as well.

"Evening, boys!" He looked me up and down. "I must say you're all looking very smart tonight." He led us to his car. I got to sit in the front.

When we arrived at the cinema he bought us all pop and a hot dog each which can't have been cheap. On the way back he asked us all about our homes, families, likes and dislikes, which lessons we liked the best; of course, we all said English, even though Luke hated it. It was so nice to be able to talk freely with a real grown-up who found us interesting and I had had such a great night I began to feel quite sad that we were going back to school and it that it would be business as usual tomorrow. Luke and Joe had been on their best behaviour the whole night, although Joe did admit to drawing a cock on the steamed-up back window of the car with his finger.

As I lay in bed that night I felt quite sorry for the English teacher. He was a nice old bloke who clearly didn't fit in with the rest of the teachers there. I didn't know if he had ever been married but I figured he must have a lonely life cooped up in his tiny flat with no-one to talk to apart from a load of annoying kids. As I drifted off to sleep I made a conscious decision to try to be less of a twat in his company from that day on.

Chapter 13

There were twins in the same year as me. They were both red haired and portly. Ordinarily this would have been enough for them both to be attacked on a regular basis. What stopped this from happening was the fact that they were psychopaths. They never left each other's side and they regularly assaulted anybody that was found alone. They were known only as the Ginger Bullies. The only other person to be seen in their presence was known as Clock, due to him having one arm shorter than the other. Clock was rated as the hardest kid in our year. He seemed to like having a pair of pet nutters.

One Sunday morning I was with the Church of England kids on my way down the country lane to church. I deeply regretted lying to the headmaster during my initial interview, telling him that I was C of E to get out of going to church every week. I envied the Catholics. They got a nice walk down to the village while the rest of us had to stay at school with the happy clappers. A leisurely walk into the village to sing a few good old-fashioned hymns was infinitely preferable to reading from an overhead projector, singing about how Jesus wanted me for a bloody sunbeam.

It was late September and I dawdled behind the other kids looking in the bushes for blackberries. I looked ahead and noticed that the Ginger Bullies had stopped and were waiting for me to catch up. One of them was brandishing a stick. Great.

"Oy, Stonekicker!" one of them called. "Where are all of your mates? Oh, I forgot, you haven't got any." They both seemed to find this comment hilarious.

"Very funny," I said.

"You what?" he replied. "Did you just call my brother a Cunt?"

"Unless you managed to read my mind, the answer's no, I didn't."

"Think you're fucking funny, do ya?" He shoved me hard in the chest while his brother stood waving his stick about.

I tripped and fell backwards into the hedge. The one with the stick then smashed it against my shins. I nearly bit through my tongue, but succeeded in not crying out. One of them used his not inconsiderable weight to hold me down while the other emptied my pockets. We had all been instructed to bring ten pence each to put in the church collection. He found this along with about fifty pence of my pocket money then got off me. The other brother kicked me hard in the ribs and they walked off laughing. I staggered to my feet and walked on down to the church.

Halfway through the service the collection plate was passed around. Luke passed it to me and I grabbed a fistful of coins from it and put them in my pocket.

"Ahh," whispered Luke. "You'll go to hell for that!"

"It's alright," I said. "I'm a Catholic. It doesn't count if you robbing from the opposition."

Chapter 14

Friday night. December. Winter of an adolescent malcontent.

You'd have thought with this many witnesses that he wouldn't be able to get away with it. That he wouldn't have the guile to even try. But he did try and he did get away with it. Plenty of times. Fear can stitch together the loosest of lips. These were different times.

I remember lying in the dormitory watching the snow falling outside. It was not the sounds of the other thirty boys snoring and farting that deprived me of sleep, rather the dread of the door at the end of the dorm opening. The housemaster's quarters were on the other side of it. The rest of the teachers would be down at the village pub. I would often hear their drunken singing in the middle of the night when they returned. The housemaster rarely joined them. So far I had never been chosen by him. I didn't know if that was luck or just that I was not one of the special ones. By the light of the moon coming through the window I could see that I was not the only one still awake. The boy in the bed next to me was lying on his back staring at the ceiling. He kept rubbing his eyes fighting to stay awake.

It was 11 o'clock at night and I knew it wouldn't be much longer. I only had a small inkling of what went on behind that door but I did know that I would never, *never* go willingly to the other side of it. I gripped the Swiss army knife tightly in my sweating palm. Whether I would find the courage to use it if the time came I didn't know. I did know that there was no other solution to the problem. God forbid I speak to an adult about it. I would be punished severely for making up such sick accusations. Derision and ostracism would be the least of my problems. My head would be well and truly above the parapet. I would be noticed by the monsters. The housemaster was not alone. I was too young to appreciate the repercussions of my actions if push came to shove, but on those dark, cold nights my survival instinct was all-consuming. I was struggling to stay awake.

I looked at the door. The light coming under it had suddenly changed. He was there. I could picture him standing with his ear to the door, trying to tell if we were all asleep. The teachers regularly patrolled the dormitories at night time to ensure we were not misbehaving. They would shine their torches at random faces and occasionally pull back the blankets to see if we had stuffed our beds with rolled up clothes to make them look occupied.

The door opened. There was no torch. He knew what he wanted. He was discreet enough not to advertise his presence. He wedged the door open with a slipper to stop it from slamming shut and crept unsteadily down the aisle between the two rows of beds. I wasn't tired anymore. I quickly swapped the knife over to my left hand in order to wipe the sweat from my palm onto my pyjama bottoms. My bed was situated towards the far end of the dorm. He continued to creep closer and closer. I closed my eyes to feign sleep, gripping the knife tighter under the blanket. The floorboards stopped creaking. I could hear his breathing and smell the booze on him. He was close. I sneaked a glance; he was in the space between my bed and the next. He turned towards the next bed. Thank God, I thought, sparing no thought for the boy who was also pretending to be asleep. He tenderly shook him by the shoulder to wake him. Without a sound the boy rose and followed him back through the door. The housemaster removed the slipper that was holding the door open and glanced up to check for witnesses. His eyes locked onto mine. We stared at each other for what felt like an eternity before he gently pulled the door shut. I breathed.

    I was awoken at about five am by one of the bedwetters getting up to go and clean his sodden bedding. In the dim morning light I watched as he tiptoed out of the dormitory, heading outside for the ablution block in the hope that no-one had witnessed his accident. I couldn't remember his name. Everybody else just called him 'Slash'. They all knew. I looked back at the door. It no longer gripped me with dread. I got back into bed and stole a glance at the bed next to mine. The boy was awake staring at me. The hostility in his eyes was palpable. Ah well, I thought. Rather you than me mate.

Chapter 15

Two hours later I was rudely awoken by a snowball in the face. It was Saturday. No classes. I was ecstatic. I still had Saturday morning games to contend with unfortunately. In this weather the prospect of standing on the snow-covered football pitch in shorts and t-shirt held no allure whatsoever. But with the thought of my free afternoon and evening to look forward to, well, I could handle just about anything.

On the way to the pitch I asked the boy what had happened. He told me that because he came top in the Maths test he had been allowed to go and watch the late horror film on the housemaster's telly. He then told me that if I mentioned a word of it to anyone he would kick my face in. Fair enough, I thought. Just as well I was shit at Maths though.

After spending ninety minutes cupping my balls to keep my hands warm while nobody passed me the football I was ready for a nice hot shower. Unfortunately it wasn't the pleasurable experience that it should have been. We were herded through like cattle with the teacher calling our names, telling us to get out after less than a minute of getting in there. I didn't like the way he seemed to recognise us by our tackle either.

After lunch I traipsed through the snow to the hedgerow at the bottom of the football field. On those rare moments when I could get some time to myself, I would regularly visit this place.

I had always loved wildlife and had aspirations to be a vet. Unfortunately I had also been a fan of Tom and Jerry cartoons and as a result had a fascination for mousetraps. I'd gone and bought one from the hardware store in the village for a pound. I'd been waiting for about an hour when a field mouse caught a whiff of the cheese I had placed in it. It got closer. I'd never seen a wild mouse before and it took my breath away. I watched it tentatively sniff the air and creep towards the trap. It stepped on to the wooden platform and nibbled at the cheese; the bar swung down and broke its neck instantly. I burst into tears then made my way back to the dorm. As I approached the school yard I saw the bed wetter kicking a stone in the yard.

"Are you ok?" he asked. I kicked him in the balls, turned and walked straight into the Geography teacher. His weapon of choice was usually the T-Square but on this occasion he dragged me straight to the headmaster.

Chapter 16

Later in the day during the punishment, I fell into a bit of a reverie. It was to become one of my harshest and fondest memories. Following a punch in the face and six of the strap from the headmaster, I had been given what would turn out to be six weeks of clearing snow from all of the paths and roads in the boarding school grounds. It wasn't my first punishment and certainly wasn't going to be my last.

As far as the punishment was concerned I should have been grateful. There were a lot worse things a child could suffer at the hands of the teachers. I'd got off lightly.

As I scraped and dug, occasionally hitting stones that sent agonising shockwaves though the shovel to my frostbitten, gloveless hands, I would glance up to chart my progress through the periscopic hood of my snorkel coat. With every backwards glance through the late afternoon gloom I would see that I had not achieved as much as my optimistic mind had hoped for. The story of my life, according to the school reports. I was bitter but found it hard to disagree with them. But I remember. Just once. Looking up from my labour I could see the hills in the distance. Nothing between us but miles of snow. The duskiness and threat of the fast approaching night cast an azure hue over the landscape. It would have made an exquisite Christmas card scene. Nocturnal creatures were beginning to brave the elements. Rabbits in a nearby field and what appeared to be a fox in the distance were taking tentative steps into the snow laden meadows. The lights of a faraway farmhouse were now visible in the gloom. The house itself casting a long shadow across the field and, for a brief moment in time, the sun and moon hung in the sky together.

The pain and the cold vanished. The experience affected me deeply. It made me realise that if I could be moved to tears by something as simple as this, then there must be a part of me that loves. It was the defining moment of my life. I began to heal and grow.

Hours later I had almost completed the task of clearing a path from the staff room to the headmaster's cottage. Night had fallen and it was only the light from the cottage that enabled me to see. I was looking at life through new eyes. I was both shamed by my actions and humbled by the realisation that although I was but a blot on this magnificent landscape, I had the power to actually add something positive as a form of gratitude for being a part of this beautiful world. I had found a part of my soul that embraced this land and finally respected everything in it. I felt hope. I peeked through the window of the cottage and glimpsed the headmaster sitting in his armchair by a dying fire smoking his pipe. The temperature had plummeted and my feet were stinging with cold. I longed to change places with the old man. I walked to the door of the cottage, turned and peed the word 'ARSE' into the snow before slowly making my way back to the dormitory. I still had quite a way to go.

Chapter 17

February came and the snow was still heavy on the ground. As I kicked the snow off my shoes and walked into the dining hall for breakfast I passed the Duty Teacher's table and the heavenly smell of fresh coffee hit my nostrils. I had an instant pang of homesickness. I'd learned to love good coffee from an early age. On freezing cold mornings when I lived with my grandparents I would always wake up to the smell coming from the percolator. I became a convert, always associating good coffee with the love and warmth when the world outside was so harsh and unforgiving.

I got to the table and made myself a drink. The coffee that we were given was instant and tasted like cigarette ash.

Later that night when Luke and Joe woke me to go on our regular nocturnal escapades we broke into the kitchen. I hunted high and low until I eventually found the stash of coffee reserved for the teachers. It was contained in small silver tins and looked grand. I opened the tins and emptied about a dozen of them into a Tupperware box that I had brought along. When we returned to the dormitory our beds were still stuffed and I knew we had got away with our crime undiscovered.

The next morning I took a small pouch of the coffee to breakfast with me. As I spooned it into my cup and added hot water my mouth was watering. It didn't mix. It just floated to the top of the cup. I tried to drink it but the bits of crunchy coffee were intolerable. I was gutted. There was no way I'd be able to steal a percolator to brew it properly without getting caught. My elaborate, perfectly executed crime had been in vain. At the end of breakfast the teacher stood and banged his cup on the table.

"It has come to my attention that somebody has stolen coffee from the kitchen. When you return to your dormitories I want you all to lay out the contents of your bedside lockers on your beds ready for inspection. Your housemasters will be posted at the door to ensure that the culprit can't escape to hide his ill-gotten gains. Now off you go!" I panicked. The tub of coffee was hidden in my locker inside the Tupperware container.

I ran through the snow back to the dormitory intent on beating everybody else. I would hide the container under Stig's bed. He was a bully and deserved it as far as I was concerned. I would feel no remorse at dropping him right in it. As I reached the dorm I noticed the housemaster waiting at the door.

"In a hurry are we?" he asked.

"I need the toilet sir," I said hurriedly.

"The ablution block is over there," he pointed out. "You're going in the wrong direction."

"Er, I need to get my toothbrush as well sir. I feel a bit sick and want to get the taste out of my mouth."

"Very well. Hurry up then, you've got inspection in ten minutes."

I hurried inside and went straight to by locker. I heard a noise behind me and turned to see the housemaster scrutinising my every move. I'd blown it. I resignedly got my toothbrush and headed to the ablution, stood idling for a couple of minutes and returned to the dormitory. By this time all of the other boys had returned and were busy laying their kit out on the bed ready for inspection. There was no way I was going to be able to hide the coffee without being spotted. I suddenly had another bright idea. I surreptitiously bent down and hid the container behind my back. When I was sure nobody was looking directly at me I casually stretched my arm out of the window behind my bed and tipped out the coffee. I gave the container a little shake to shake loose the stubborn bits and brought my arm back inside and placed it on my bed with the rest of my kit ready for inspection. Nobody noticed a thing.

The inspection soon followed and was completed with the housemaster looking somewhat dejected having not found the culprit. As I walked down to the assembly hall I felt like a huge weight had been lifted.

I had been chosen to do the morning's Bible reading after hymns. I had no qualms about doing this. I fancied myself as quite the raconteur, capable of adding an over-dramatic flare to the otherwise dull-as-dishwater content and secretly enjoyed the attention. I finished my reading and returned to the crowd. As we were about to commence prayers the housemaster entered the hall and approached the headmaster. He whispered furtively in his ear and went and stood by the door. The headmaster looked at me.

"I'd just like to say that I thought you'd done a splendid job of this morning's bible reading," he said. I blushed as all eyes turned to me. "I would be grateful if you would stay behind after assembly so I could have a quiet word."

I was gobsmacked; he'd never spoken a kind word to me before. I must have done a good job. I wasn't sure I liked the smile he gave me though. I dutifully waited until everybody else had left before I approached the head. Out of the corner of my eye I noticed the housemaster grinning by the door.

"If you would just accompany your housemaster I'd be very grateful," said the head. I walked over to him.

"Follow me," he said and walked out into the snow in the direction of the dormitory.

"Where are we going sir?"

"Just follow me," he said mysteriously. As we approached the dormitory he stopped and pointed. "See that?" he asked.

I looked towards the dormitory with growing dismay. Underneath what could only be my window the snow had turned into a huge mound of brown slush where the coffee had landed.

"Yes sir."

"You bloody idiot," he said shaking his head. "I trust you're not going to make things worse by denying it, are you?"

"No sir," I replied. He's right, I thought. I am a bloody idiot.

Amazingly, I wasn't strapped, slippered or caned for my crime. I guessed that all of the teaching staff found the whole incident quite amusing. I was, however, given snow clearing duties again. This ended up lasting for about a fortnight. I also had to sacrifice my pocket money to pay for the coffee to be replaced. That hurt. I only had forty pence a week and it would take until summer for them to fully recoup the cost. Still, I was looking forward to the snow clearing. It had only been about three weeks since my last snow clearing punishment had expired and I curiously missed it.

Chapter 18

I sat at my desk looking at the window, not out of it but at it. It was raining heavily and I gazed at the streaks it made down the window, at the patterns that formed. The fogginess of it. The glistening cobweb in the corner of the window pane shook in the wind, sending rain, like teardrops, to the sill below. The spider, clinging on for dear life, waited patiently at the sidelines, longing for a better day when the flies wouldn't be so shy and he could patrol his web without fear of being ripped away.

The board rubber missed my head and cracked the glass.

"Wake up!" shouted the head.

"I wasn't asleep, sir," I replied.

"See me after class." The familiar phrase everybody dreaded.

I spent the rest of the lesson with my eyes front, pretending to listen to whatever it was that the old bastard was rattling on about. His threats didn't bother me one iota by now. The pain was always fleeting. His arsenal was full of blanks as far as I was concerned. There were many that were terrified of the prospect of 'six of the best' and who would live the rest of their lives haunted by the sound of a cane whistling through the air towards them; I wasn't one of them. True, I detested the man and most of his colleagues, but not out of fear. They were less than human. They would preach in assembly about God and the good deeds of Jesus and angels and forgiveness and shit, then follow on from that by behaving like the Devil himself, tormenting and beating and, apparently, sodomising those in their care. The hypocrisy stunk. The fact that none of them had ever seemingly been plagued by self doubt or harboured anything less than resentment towards the boys made me hate them all the more and wonder what the hell they were doing in the job. I guess they were just pissed on power.

More than anything, anything, I just wanted people to leave me alone. Looking at the stormy weather outside reminded me of Brighton, of being on my own on the beach, being battered by those waves. I had never felt as alive and happy as I had on those days when nothing and nobody bothered me, when I didn't have to calculate and scheme just to exist, when I didn't have to worry about what the next day had in store for me, when I was innocent and the simplest of experiences like getting wet would make my spirits soar.

I had never felt tired before, but I was tired now. I just wanted something other than this, this life. I didn't know what it was or how to get it but I just knew that I didn't want another second of this. I had to do something to get out of here. But I was tired.

The cobweb and spider were gone, battered into oblivion by forces outside of their control. The crack in the window was all too apparent. As the wind attacked it, it had spread. Then I spotted the spider. It had survived. I watched it crawl back into the corner of the window pane to wait out the storm. I looked down at the board rubber lying on the floor and began to feel revitalised. You missed, I thought. Was that the best you could do?

Chapter 19

One Easter holiday the best thing happened to me. I contracted Chicken Pox! I couldn't believe my luck. If it had happened at school I would have been confined to the Sick Bay. As it was I had to stay at home until I was totally clear. The spots and scabs itched like buggery and I wasn't allowed out of the flat but I was in heaven. I managed to pass it on to my mum's boyfriend. He wasn't quite as pleased as me to contract chicken pox as his lead to shingles and severe scarring.

I stayed at home for a whole fortnight after the other kids had gone back to school. Although it interfered with my mum's studying she still managed to wait on me and feed me a steady supply of library books.

We lived in a ground floor council flat on the rough side of town. It was the kind of place where you had to get your milk bottles in the second you heard the milk float or else the milk would be stolen or worse. We all overslept one day and opened the front door to find a bottle with the milk replaced with a human turd.

One night my mum decided to go to the cinema. Although I had chicken pox I wasn't ill and I was old enough to look after myself for a couple of hours. I had a warm blanket and drinks and snacks to enjoy in front of the television. I had just nodded off in the armchair when there was an almighty crash. I flew backwards in the chair out of shock, hit my head on the table knocking everything off and landed on the floor. I jumped up to determine what had happened and saw that the large living room window had been shattered and there was a house brick in the middle of the carpet. I panicked, not knowing what to do. I kept my head low, in case there was going to be another missile thrown my way. I didn't want to call the police because I wasn't sure where my mum stood legally, leaving me on my own. I decided that my great aunt would be the best person to call. She was the only person whose number I remembered. Luckily we had recently had a telephone fitted so I didn't have to get dressed and leave the flat in a vulnerable state.

After getting a taxi (she couldn't drive) she arrived about half an hour later. Relief flooded through me. I had imagined all sorts of horrible things happening to me while I was stuck there on my own. I had heard nothing since the window had been smashed but was convinced that there was a gang out there that was slowly creeping towards the flat to get me. My aunt deemed it prudent to call the police despite my protestations that my mum might get in trouble. As it turned out there was nothing to worry about. The police listened to my account of what had happened and left. My aunt stayed with me until my mum got back from the cinema.

The experience made me almost appreciate boarding school. I spent the rest of my recovery period lying in bed terrified that a brick could land on my head at any given moment or that the window would shatter and hands would reach down and drag me out. I felt quite relieved when I had to go back to school where the things to be afraid of at least had recognisable faces.

Chapter 20

The school had originally been built as a temporary fixture to house children who had been evacuated from the city during the bombings in World War 2. All things considered then, it was ironic that there was no 'Spirit of the Blitz' apparent among the children.

There was plenty of fun to be had amid all this misery. I say fun, but it was more schadenfreude. I felt slightly blessed and thankful when it wasn't me that was under attack. But that always cut both ways.

I was sitting in History one day, listening to the teacher regale us with tales of the war. We had quickly realised that if we asked him about his experiences fighting the 'nazzies' as he put it, he would spend the rest of the lesson bragging thus limiting the amount of class and homework that we could be given. I actually felt quite relaxed during this lesson. The knowledge that after the war he had become an ordained minister gave me some comfort. Despite the fact that every morning we had bible readings in assembly and every weekend we had some form of religious activity, the school had seemed to me to be bereft of any kindness. In my naivety I believed that kindness was at the heart of Christianity. The fact that we had a real 'Man of God' in our school reassured me that goodness could be found here. He was of a certain age, an age where frequent visits to the toilet were a necessity. Kids often dared each other to spit in his trilby during his absences. It relieved the boredom. I was one of those kids who rarely had the nerve to initiate any of these deeds but thought that the naughtiness of others was both fascinating and hilarious. It was therefore all the more terrifying when I was dared to do the deed. Although inwardly petrified, I grinned, stood and made my way to the front of the class. I leant over the hat, hawked and let go a huge globule of phlegm. It was a particularly stringy one that refused to let go of my bottom lip. I heard the door open and tried in vain to suck it back into my mouth. The teacher screamed at me. He made me stand with my hand out while he positioned a chair close to where I was standing.

"Wait there," he ordered and left the room.

The waiting was the worst thing. I wasn't particularly bothered by the beatings the teachers gave me. I had had a lot worse from my dad. This time though, it upset me. I had been lulled into believing that this man wasn't like the rest. The betrayal of that faith I had in him cut to the quick. He returned to the room with a very impressive looking cane that was about three feet long with a curved handle. He then shocked me by standing on his chair while ordering me, again, to stay still. He then leapt off his chair with a ferocious snarl and brought the cane down as hard as he could. The cane whistled through the air as it came down towards my outstretched hand. Sod this, I thought and whipped my hand away just in time which caused him to land on the floor without being able to pull back the cane in time. The crack as he hit himself on the shin made me wince. The rest of the class howled as the teacher dropped his cane and grabbed his leg to sooth the pain. I didn't think it was so funny. Things will only deteriorate from here, I thought. I was right. When he had regained his posture he administered six of the cane on each of my hands. No-one had ever seen him give more than four before. He made sure to leave a gap of about five seconds between each strike to ensure that the pain fully registered. His face was bright red and he was sweating profusely by the end of it all. Although my hands were bleeding and beginning to discolour and my illusions about men of the cloth had been shattered, I was quite proud of the fact that I was now a record breaker.

Later that afternoon I was excused P.E. It was obvious that I wouldn't be able to hold a rounders bat. I sat nursing my bloodied, swollen hands. It occurred to me that I was cursed. In a moment of clarity I realised that I had never in my life actually got away with anything. Every bad deed I had committed had been found out.

I thought back to the one and only time my mother had hit me. I was about six years old and I had been out playing with some of the kids from the council estate that we lived on. My mother was being visited by the Saucepan Man, a salesman who regularly visited the estate to sell, well, saucepans. I was dared by the other boys to swear through the letterbox of the high-rise flat we lived in. I remember shaking with a mixture of fear and excitement as I bent down and opened the letterbox with my thumb. I didn't know many swear-words at the time, only the ones that I heard my dad use. Although every other word he uttered was a profanity for some reason my mind had gone blank and there was only one that I could remember. I took a deep breath.

"Shit!" I shouted, and turned to flee down the stairs. I was too slow. The door flung open and my mother grabbed me by the scruff of the neck and pulled me into the flat as the other boys legged it. In front of the Saucepan Man she pulled my pants down, smacked me on the backside and sent me to the bedroom I shared with my brother. My brother had watched the whole incident with a smug look on his face.

As I sat there reminiscing I vowed never to again be the perpetrator of any wrongdoing. Unfortunately I forgot this vow within an hour.

After classes had finished I made my way to the storeroom where we all kept our tuck-boxes. Being a fussy eater there were only a couple of days a week that I actually ate my tea; today was not one of those days. For the third time that week I decided to pick the locks of some of the other boxes to see what I could find. I removed the paper clip from my pocket and started looking for the right kind of lock. The chunky, colourful ones were usually the easiest. My hands were still smarting and were considerably stiff but within five minutes I'd got one open. It was Stig's.

Stig was an animal. But theft of his tuck didn't occur to me as an act of revenge, a strike for the underdogs. I would just have happily devoured the contents of the smallest boy's box. The box was full. There were biscuits, crisps, chocolate spread, peanut butter and multiple bars of chocolate. I took the lot. It wouldn't all fit in my impenetrable box so I stuffed the rest into my pockets.

My tuck-box was a small grey wooden one with my name painted on it in white that had originally been used as an ammunition box, according to my dad. I thought that was pretty cool. Most of the other boys had big metal toolboxes. I wasn't jealous; my box was my most treasured possession. Yes, you could fit more into the toolboxes, but that didn't bother me. I had plenty of hiding places for my plunder.

I returned to the dorm and sat on my bed chomping away at bar of chocolate with Spanish writing on it. It wasn't as nice as English chocolate but it would do. I was about halfway through it when Stig walked up to my bed.

"What are you eating?" he asked.

"Chocolate."

"Give me some or I'll break your nose," he said.

Being only a second year half his size I felt it prudent to give him some. Recognition dawned on his face.

"Where did you get this?"

"My mum brought it back from Torremolinos," I replied.

"I've got some of these, they're alright aren't they?"

"Not bad," I replied. He grunted and walked away.

I made my way to the dining hall for tea feeling more than a little bit worried. It was only a matter of time before he discovered his empty tuck-box and put two and two together.

It turned out I didn't have to wait long. I was on supper duty that night. This involved going to the kitchen and collecting the jugs of squash, beakers and biscuits. I had to bring them back to the dorm and issue a drink and two biscuits to everybody under the watchful eye of the house captain who usually helped himself to anybody else's. I was walking back carefully carrying a tower of beakers when I was ambushed. As I entered the lobby I was shoved into the radiator against a wall. The knob had come off the ventilation lever and it punctured my back. I fell to the floor and curled into a ball as three pairs of feet kicked the crap out of me. After a couple of minutes the kicking stopped. I didn't feel any pain but I was aware of the blood that poured down my back.

"Touch my stuff again and I will fucking kill you, do you hear me you fucking weirdo?"

I groaned. There was another sharp kick to my ribs. I felt something give. They left. I looked up and saw that the beakers were scattered across the floor. I began to stack them again when Mr McEwan the English teacher who happened to be on duty that night walked in.

Mr McEwan was the only teacher in the school that I

really liked. He was short and quite fat pushing sixty. He had a thick head of grey hair that had a browny yellow streak going through it that I believed was a result of the pipe he never had out of his mouth. He had huge gnarled fingers that had been 'bust up by the bloody Japs'. He never caned us if we got less than half marks in a test; he always showed a real interest in my work and regularly praised me for my essays. On the occasional Saturday afternoon he would take me and one other boy to town to watch a cricket match. He would buy us ice-creams and explain the rules of the game. I didn't actually like cricket, the ball scared me, but these trips meant a lot. He was a good person.

"Jesus, what happened? Are you alright?" he asked.

"Yes sir. I fell over," I replied.

"Come on, let's get you to Sick bay," he sighed despondently as he gently picked me up.

After an examination by the matron it was determined that my puncture wound did not require stitches, but that I had dislodged a floating rib and would remain in the Sick-bay overnight. Mr McEwan stayed to make sure I was alright. He tried to glean more information from me, but I wasn't forthcoming. I knew where that would get me. Before he left he brought me a mug of cocoa and some biscuits. That night was the first that I didn't dream of being somewhere else.

Chapter 21

One night just before lights out, Odd Bod shouted across the dorm to me.

"How old are you, Stonekicker?"

"Fourteen and eleven twelfths," I replied. Having my birthday in August meant that I was the youngest in the year. When it came to toughness and maturity every month mattered.

"You a virgin then?" he asked.

"No, I shagged a girl on the school cruise," I lied.

"He did," lied Joe. "I was there." I was quite moved by Joe's support.

"Fair do's. What about you, Bonehead?" he asked the unfortunate looking boy who had a face so thin and pale and with skin so taut it looked like a living skull.

"Does a cat count?" he asked genuinely.

"No it doesn't, you fucking freak. What d'you want to come out with shit like that for?"

"It's true," protested Bonehead. "About a year ago when my mum went down the shops, I gave my cat one. Tried to scratch the fuck out of me but I just forced its head down and I managed it.

"Right, quieten down you lot," called out the Geography teacher who happened to be on duty that night. "Lights out in two minutes, and I do not want to hear a peep."

I think that more than a few of us had strange dreams that night, and we all became rather wary of Bonehead afterwards. There were some things even *we* struggled to take the piss out of.

Later that night I received what was now a familiar tap on the shoulder by Joe to get up and go and do some mischief. We all quietly stuffed our beds as usual and with Luke leading the way with his torch we snuck out of the dormitory and headed for the staff dining room.

"Do you think Bonehead really did that?" I asked.

"God knows," replied Luke. "He told me once that he dug his dead dad up in the graveyard."

"Why would he do that?" asked Joe.

"Dunno. I think he just likes showing off."

"I can't see him winning over too many admirers coming out with shit like that," I said.

"Yeah, they should have called *him* Stonekicker. Doesn't it bother you; everybody calling you that, making out you're some sort of Billy-no-mates?" asked Luke.

"Not being funny mate, but I'd say your nickname is just a bit more offensive than mine. Besides, I've always believed you've got to respect somebody's opinion to be offended by it, and as I think they're all tossers, I'm really not that bothered what they call me," I said.

"We call you Stonekicker too," said Luke. "Does that mean we're tossers?"

"Yep."

We arrived at the dining hall. We came here at night to raid the kitchens, but tonight's plan to do the staff dining room was, we felt, our most ambitious expedition to date. We got out the cutlery we had stashed and while two of us prized open the sash window of the kitchen half an inch, Luke slid a knife into the gap we had made and popped the latch. I then gave Joe a bunk-up so he could climb through and open the door for us. We ignored the goods on offer in the kitchen, walked out of the door to the dining room and through to the room that the staff ate in. It was like a treasure trove. We were only given corn flakes or bran flakes as cereal. Here there was every variety under the sun.

And there was real butter. We only had cheap margarine.

Over the years, when the teachers were in our dining hall I noticed what each of them ate. I went straight for the headmaster's cereal and started filling my face. Joe meanwhile, had put some toast in the toaster while Luke was making himself a cup of Earl Grey tea. We were that excited we had dropped our guard. Nobody was looking out of the windows. It didn't matter. A minute later Joe's toast got stuck in the toaster and smoke started billowing from it.

"Run!" I shouted.

We had just arrived at the dormitory when the alarm went off. All eyes were upon us as we dived into our beds. A second later the housemaster stormed into the dormitory in his dressing gown and slippers and ordered us all to go straight to the playground for a roll check.

One of the older boys came up to me as we were on our way.

"What the fucking hell have you been playing at?" he asked me.

"You're not going to grass us up are you?" I asked him.

"I'm not, but I can't vouch for the rest of them. The whole dorm saw you come in as the alarm went off."

As the roll call was carried out I watched with growing trepidation as the History teacher made his way over from the direction of the dining hall. He walked straight up to the deputy head, Fat Dog, and whispered in his ear.

"It appears that some boys have been helping themselves to food from the staff dining room," Fat Dog shouted across the yard. Laugher and gossip broke out amongst the ranks. "Quiet!" he bellowed. "The alarm you all heard was the result of somebody burning toast. Not only is this a blatant act of disrespect towards the teaching staff, it is a breach of the school rules and is also extremely dangerous and irresponsible. Fortunately, the dining hall has not burnt down, but the fire brigade have had to be summoned. Now, we are all going to stand here until somebody owns up."

Everybody groaned. I looked across at Luke and Joe who were both silent and pale-faced. I waited. I felt all eyes were on me. There was no way any of us were going to put our hands up to the deed, but I just knew somebody would tell on us. None of us were what anybody would call popular.

After fifteen minutes of silence, it remarkably became apparent that we were not going to be grassed up. I was amazed. It was also obvious that the teachers' resilience to the elements had nothing on that of the pupils. They were all shivering and muttering to themselves despondently.

"Right," Fat Dog called. "Everybody back to your dormitories, but whoever did this, believe me, this is not over."

It was.

Chapter 22

The holidays flew by. Getting back on the coach in the bus station was a sombre affair. My mum was always a little sad but excited for me, saying how jealous she was of me, how she had been enthralled by Enid Blyton's 'Mallory Towers' books as a child and had always dreamed of going to boarding school.

"Do you have midnight feasts?" she once asked.

"Sort of," I replied, feeling sicker by the minute at the prospect of getting on the coach.

"Come on, cheer up. It's not as bad as you think. Look, all of your friends seem happy enough." I looked around. Sure enough most of the boys were laughing and joking with each other. The only miserable looking ones were the outcasts, the boys who were always the objects of ridicule and ignominy. I was not one of them. I wasn't. I forced a smile.

"That's better. On you get then. Christmas will be here before you know it." She leant forward to kiss me. I recoiled.

"Jesus, mum. What are you doing?" I turned, gave my suitcase to the driver and climbed up the steps onto the coach. There was still ten minutes before the coach was due to leave, so I had no problem finding a window seat. I looked at my mother and tried to make sure the longing I felt to be with her wasn't noticeable. The coach filled up. A boy tapped me on the shoulder.

"Oy, stonekicker, shift your arse so I can sit by me mate." I shrugged and moved to an aisle seat.

The boys were unruly to say the least. There was a small group of older boys at the back of the coach that were led by Stig. Whenever the coach slowed down or stopped at traffic lights they would attract the attention of passers-by, particularly the elderly, by waving angelically at them. As soon as the waves were reciprocated they would then either stick two fingers up at them or squash their bare arses against the window.

As the coach turned a sharp corner, the contents of one of the boy's bag spilled out from the overhead shelf. A pair of soiled pants fell onto the back of a seat.

"Eeargh, you dirty bastard," a boy shouted, pointing at the skid marks adorning the Y-fronts.

"It's chocolate!" the boy cried. "My chocolate melted in the bag," he pleaded to the crowd in vain. For the next four and a half years he was simply known as Skidder, skid, skiddy-pants or shitty-knickers. No good deeds ever mattered or were remembered; it was our less fortunate actions that would always define us. I wanted to just close my eyes and imagine being somewhere else, but I daren't for fear of having something shoved up my nose.

I looked down the aisle and noticed that all three bedwetters were sitting by each other. All three had been assigned different school houses as well. Was this a conscious decision that somebody had made? And if so, then why? And did they really believe their mutual problem was something that could unify them? I spent the rest of the journey pondering these questions. It took my mind off all the other crap that I was expecting on arrival.

Chapter 23

One day I discovered something wonderful. We could actually get out of Saturday morning games and church on Sunday if we took up camping. Unfortunately we had to take a partner. On most occasions this didn't turn out too badly, but there were times when I was desperate to get back to school as the company proved insufferable. Most kids chose friends to be their partner. Those who couldn't find anybody had to team up with each other. This usually happened to me.

One Friday after school we went to collect our kit from the woodwork teacher. I had been saddled with a boy who was in the year above me and subsequently I was bound to become his slave. It dawned on me that his nickname was 'Stenchpipe' and that this didn't bode well for me as I was to spend the weekend cooped up with him in a tent. No wonder he turned up on his own for the camping trip. We were issued with a tent, flysheet, rolled up sleeping mats and bags, mess tins, ration packs and a gas stove. These were inspected by the teacher on issue and expected to be brought back in pristine condition. We were then told that we could either camp in the school paddock or venture up to the hills four miles away. Not many opted for the paddock. We were instructed to be back by teatime on Sunday, not to hitchhike, smoke or upset any of the locals.

It was pouring with rain as we walked out of the school gates but our spirits were soaring. As expected, I was made to carry the bulk of the kit but that didn't bother me. We jogged to the local shop where I was made to go in and buy ten cigarettes and a box of matches. Although younger than the other boy I was very tall for my age, so I guess it made sense. As I fearfully approached the counter I looked at the shopkeeper. She was middle aged with a tight bleached perm. She regarded me with a pained expression, leaned to the left and let out an almighty fart.

"Ooh, you must excuse me, I've got dreadful wind," she said. "What can I get you?"

I asked for the cigarettes. She could tell exactly where I was from and exploited my desperation by charging double. I came out and we put out our thumbs. After ten minutes a pick-up truck came by. The driver let us sit in the back in the open air with the potatoes and dropped us off a mile further up the road. We failed to get another lift after that. Somebody in a hatchback stopped but drove off as we got close to the car. The rain was coming down in sheets which rendered it impossible to light a fag.

We eventually reached the campsite. It was situated at the top of a big hill, half a mile from the road. We were the only ones there.

"You put the tent up while I go for a fag under that tree," said Stenchpipe.

After watching me desperately flail about in the wind and rain he realised that he'd better step in or it would be a night camping al fresco. It was getting dark and we couldn't tell the colour coordinated poles apart. We eventually succeeded in putting up something that loosely resembled a tent and climbed inside. He kindly rewarded me with one of the cigarettes that I had paid for. I'd only tried to smoke once before without much success but I'd be damned if I was going to turn down the offer and look like a sissy. After three hearty coughs I eventually got the hang of it. While he dug out the torn remnants of a porno mag from his rucksack I watched in awe as the storm tried to rip us apart. The trees were bending in the wind and the only thing that drowned out the roar of the rain on the tent roof was the growl of the approaching thunder. I was in heaven. Half an hour after pitching our tent we watched as another pair of boys arrived at the camp and struggled to put up theirs. I recognised one of them as a boy known as Indy. His name was actually Andrew but he had trouble with his reading and writing and invariably he wrote his name down as 'Indrew' hence the nickname 'Indy'. In retrospect I suppose he was dyslexic but as knowledge of the condition was in its infancy he was generally diagnosed as being some kind of half-wit.

When they had completed their equally poor job of tent erecting they both came over to our tent with their ration packs. No-one seemed fond of rhubarb so I had three huge family-sized tins to devour over the weekend. We got rid of our kidney flavoured soup and teabags and to my dismay Stenchpipe received an extra tin of baked beans.

Later that night while I was reading my book by torchlight Stenchpipe looked up from his porno mag and gave me a nudge.

"Give me a wank," he said.

"Do I have to," I replied.

"You don't *have* to, but I think you'll like it."

I bloody didn't like it. It made a mess and I felt a bit disgusted by the whole experience. Afterwards he returned to his magazine and stuck his hand back down his pants.

The 'Gentleman's literature' he was reading was entitled Hairy Twats. I doubted that it depicted idiots with beards. But I was curious. The only publications of this ilk I had encountered before had been the Page three calendar that my step grandfather used to have hidden on the top shelf of the living room cupboard before he went blind. This was something else. I only hoped he'd let me have a look at it over the weekend without getting any funny ideas.

"What are you reading about?" I asked, trying to make polite conversation.

"It's an in-depth study on the origin of the Aswan Dam."

"No it isn't," I replied.

"Of course it fucking isn't," he said. "If you must know I'm reading a story about this bored housewife that gets spit-roasted by the bin men." I didn't actually know what that meant but I didn't want to pursue the matter for fear of looking stupid. I made the decision to keep my mouth shut and go to sleep listening to the storm rage outside. Stenchpipe farted. I wondered when that was going to start, I thought, and buried my head under the sleeping bag.

The next morning I awoke after a particularly rough night. Stenchpipe had tried getting amorous in his sleep on more than one occasion and I'd frequently had to shrug him off. The hard wet floor of the tent hadn't helped much either. It was freezing and stunk to high heaven. Luckily the water hadn't seeped into my sleeping bag and for that I was grateful. I poked my head out of the tent. The bad weather had hardly abated. It was still pouring with rain and the cold wind had blown down the tent of the boys opposite. It didn't seem to have disturbed their sleep though. I could make out their bodies lying under the collapsed orange fabric. They could be dead of course, I thought, then realised with some consternation that I needed the toilet. I got myself fully dressed inside my sleeping bag as I didn't want to encourage Stenchpipe, searched the tent for the trowel and toilet paper then made my way over to the nearby trees.

"We know what you're doing, you dirty bastard," came a call from the other tent that hadn't collapsed. Oh, the shame of it all.

The rain abated. When I got back Stenchpipe had the stove on and was busy adding food to the pan.

"What have you got in there?" I asked.

"This is going to be delicious," he said while vigorously stirring the contents of the pan. A really unpleasant smell accosted my nostrils. "I've mixed up baked beans, spam, kidney soup and bits of bread."

"You'd better turn the heat down," I said. The edges of the mixture were already burnt black.

"Get your mess tin out, it's ready," he said.

"I don't think I'll bother." I was starving but there was no way I was going to eat that muck. "I'll have some rhubarb." I dug around the tent until I found the three big tins. Stenchpipe was uttering profanities and trying to rescue his breakfast as the rain came down again.

I took my food with a tin opener deep into the woods and I sat down against a tree to enjoy my meal in peace. I didn't have a spoon so I dug the chunks of rhubarb out with my fingers then drank the juice out of the tin. The rain still managed to find me beneath the canopy of the trees and my arse was drenched but it didn't bother me as I lovingly lapped up my rhubarb. Before I knew it I had devoured all three tins of the stuff and was feeling particularly uncomfortable and bloated. I stood up too quickly and, feeling dizzy, leant against the tree and threw up every last chunk. As I headed back to the camp I vowed never to touch the stuff again. I left the tins in the woods for small animals to make their nests in.

We spent the rest of the day taking turns with stenchpipe's porn and generally getting on each other's nerves. Indy insisted on blasting music from his radio while I was trying to read. Fortunately Stenchpipe, who was struggling to concentrate on a particularly juicy reader's letter in his magazine, got fed up with the incessant racket and drop-kicked the boy's radio into the woods then sat sucking his big toe until the swelling went down.

To try and quell the oppressive atmosphere I suggested we all do something about the ant problem that we were all suffering from. Ants were crawling through all of the tents, hiding in the sleeping bags and swarming over any food that was left out. I discovered that they originated from a nest on a nearby tree trunk. I got hold of a bottle of paraffin, took a swig and held it in my mouth while I struck a match. I then sprayed the paraffin out of my mouth, into the flame and incinerated the ants on the tree trunk.

"You could have blown your head off doing that, you idiot," said Stenchpipe.

"I suppose it would have been safer if you had just lit one of your farts," I said. "Still, it got the taste of that puke out of my mouth."

"Best stay off the fags until you had a drink though," he said and offered me a swig out of the bottle of shandy that I had seen one of the other boys take a sneaky piss in earlier.

"No you're alright," I said. I watched as he took a swig himself then walked off in search of a drink of water before I threw up again.

That night he tried it on again.

"Can I give it a miss?" I asked politely.

"Suit yourself," he said despondently. He took that quite well, I thought.

It was another miserable night having to endure the putrescent stink that emanated from Stenchpipe's backside, but as we made our way back to school the next day I realised that I had actually enjoyed myself in the company of the other boys. I suppose I could have done without Stenchpipe trying it on both nights but he took my declining his offer with good grace and I felt we had generally got on quite well.

When we arrived back at the school we went through the kit with the woodwork teacher and it turned out that one of us had left all of the tent pegs behind. We got the T-square twice on the backside for that but overall I felt that it had been worth it.

Chapter 24

After English, my favourite lesson was Religious Education. I had always considered myself to be pretty much agnostic so it wasn't the subject matter that appealed to me. It was the teacher: a female. The fact that she was middle-aged (at least thirty) was irrelevant; she was a woman and they were in short supply. All of the boys loved R.E. for exactly the same reason.

"I have five wanks a day fantasising about her," said Odd Bod as we were waiting to go into the lesson one day.

"I've seen her tits," said Joe.

"Have you bollocks," said Odd Bod.

"I bloody have. I was sweeping leaves for detention one day near her flat. She'd just done a cross-country run and took off her sweaty top before she noticed the curtains were open."

Odd Bod pointed at Skid.

"Eargh. Look everyone. Skid's got a bone-on."

"Shut up!" shouted Skid, who did indeed have a bone-on. I had to admit, Joe's story was a bit on the steamy side and I found myself having to think about my dead pet dog to stop myself from ending up in the same predicament as Skid.

She was coming. We all watched hungrily as she walked up the corridor and counted us into the classroom.

Although we all spent most of the time in R.E. trying to look up the teacher's skirt, we actually did a surprising amount of work. We were all desperate to please her.

"Pay attention boys," she said in her velvety, forty fags a day seductive voice. "I want you write a twenty minute essay on the subject: 'Why should Christians worship in church if God is omnipotent?'"

"What's omnipotent, miss?" asked Bonehead. Everybody made stupid noises, calling him a retard.

"Quiet!" the teacher shouted. We obeyed immediately. None of us wanted to get on her bad side. Everybody thought they were in with a chance of wooing her. I, however, quite fancied the idea of being caned across the backside by her. "Omnipotent means 'everywhere'," she said.

I knew for a fact that none of the others had a bloody clue what it meant either. Most of us knew never to ask a question in class, even if your life depended on it, but if somebody forgot this cardinal rule it was only right that they were brutally reminded not to do it again. I looked at the question. I didn't have a clue why Christians worshipped in church. Ask them, I thought. I started to write something about it being good to listen to vicars but my mind soon wandered. I looked around. Everybody had slid down in their chairs, trying to catch a glimpse of the teacher's knickers while she was busy marking books. I slid down and sneaked a peek myself. No good, she had her legs crossed.

The twenty minutes seemed to go on forever. I'd only written about five lines. Well, that'll have to do, I thought. I ripped a piece of paper out of my book and wrote a message to Skid. 'Have you still got a *stiffy*?' I screwed up the bit of paper, attached a paper clip to aid its projection and flicked it at him with my ruler. It hit him in the side of the face. He yelped. I couldn't believe the wimp. It can't have hurt and besides, I was only trying to get him to look over at my note.

"What on earth's going on?" shouted the teacher.

"Stonekicker just flicked something at me, miss," he blurted.

"We call people by their god given surnames in here," she said to him, then turned her attention to me. I couldn't believe she knew who he was talking about. Did the teachers secretly call me that as well? The bastards! "Come here, she said, "and bring the piece of paper that he flicked at you."

Oh God, I thought. She took it from Skid's hand and read it. Her face went crimson.

"This is obscene," she said, but she wouldn't read it out. She screwed it up and put it in the bin. "Put your hand out." She grabbed her cane from behind the desk and gave me one lash on each hand. "Go back to your seat. I want a hundred lines from you tomorrow entitled 'I must not disrupt the Religious Education classes.'"

"Can I write R.E. for short, miss?" I asked.

"No."

I returned to my seat with mixed emotions. I was annoyed that I had been grassed up and punished but I was also quite excited about the fact that the teacher had caned me as it had been a bit of a fantasy of mine. It was a shame it wasn't on the backside. That really would have made it all worthwhile.

Chapter 25

There was a boy in our year that really should not have been at the school. He was, to coin a popular phrase used by the boys, a retard. He had the rather unfortunate nickname of 'Windowlicker', apparently a reference to way the mentally handicapped appear on buses. He could not spell his own name, he was friendly and trusting of everyone, he played with toy soldiers and he came last in every subject. He was also fat, useless at sports and wet the bed. He was eaten alive by staff and pupils alike. Within a week of his arrival he had lost most of his belongings.

I would often look across the school yard and see him being taunted and hit by the other kids. I couldn't watch for long.

I saw him in the dormitory one day, sitting on his own playing with his toy soldiers. When it was time to go for dinner he carefully placed them all in a shoe box and put them in his bedside cabinet. I waited for him to leave the dormitory before I stole them.

Weeks later he caught me looking at them on my bed.

"I like your soldiers," he commented. "I used to have some like that." He looked longingly at the plastic figures in my lap. I felt a small stab of guilt.

"You can buy them off me if you like," I said.

"Yes please," he said enthusiastically. "How much do you want for them?"

"Give me your weekly pocket money until the end of term and I'll let you have them now."

He beamed. It was a deal.

Chapter 26

One year my mum had managed to save enough money for me to go on the school cruise. There were about twenty of us and we were accompanied by the headmaster and his wife. Joe had managed to persuade his parents into letting him go, so I knew that if we had to pair up at times it wouldn't be too traumatic. My mum was really excited for me and encouraged me to keep a diary while I was away for the fortnight.

We flew to Yugoslavia where we were to board the ship. There were about thirty other schools joining us on the cruise and it soon became apparent that we were the only ones who had to wear school uniform at all times. We were all taken to the cabins which would be our home for the next two weeks. Four of us had to share with some older German boys as we could not all fit in one cabin. There was no window or décor in ours, just four metal bunk beds and grey linoleum on the floor. I must admit, it looked a bit more glamorous in the brochure. I guessed that was where the teachers were accommodated.

We introduced ourselves to the Germans, who spoke a damn sight better English than we spoke German, then unpacked and went up to meet the others on the deck as we set sail. The headmaster informed us that he had been lucky enough to acquire the use of a small conference room so that we could have classes in between stops. That wasn't in the brochure either. We were then given an hour to explore the ship before tea. I ran straight to the aft of the ship to watch as we went out to sea. I was elated. It was the first time I had ever been abroad. The alien sights and smells and languages fascinated me. A group from another school came and stood by me to watch as we left the port. I noticed a girl of about my age whose beauty took my breath away. She was tall and had long, curly brown hair with almond shaped eyes and freckles on her nose. I was in love. Girls were as alien to me as the country I was in, and even more captivating and mysterious. Joe came up to me.

"What are you staring at?" he asked.

"Nothing. I'm just watching the shore."

"Bollocks. You fancy one of those girls, don't you?"

"Will you shut up, they'll hear you."

"Which one?" he whispered.

"I wish you'd fuck off," I said.

"I reckon I could get off with her," he said, indicating a small plump girl with short blond hair who happened to be chatting to the girl that had caught my eye. Although we were desperate and looked total twats in our school uniforms, I liked to think that I could set my sights slightly higher than Joe, who just seemed prepared to opt for the most attainable.

"Go for it," I said. It could be a way in for me too, I thought.

"Maybe tomorrow," he said. "Gives us a chance to settle in and suss out the rest of the talent."

"Shit-out. Come on, let's go for tea."

The following day we arrived at the Greek island of Santorini. Many many years ago this island had been a live volcano that erupted and killed zillions. It was now extinct and what was left of the volcano was inhabited by a thriving community who lived on its plateau. To get to the town above from the harbour it was necessary to ride a donkey and zigzag up a steep narrow pathway that was cut into the side of the volcano. I looked up and could see the donkeys leisurely making their way up. Due to the large crowd disembarking, it seemed that they had to dip into their reserve pool of beasts. The donkey I had been given to ride was about half my size and frothed at the mouth. Trying to avoid its rabid bite, I climbed onto its back. As soon as my arse touched the saddle it bolted off up the side of the volcano and crashed into the two foot high wall that was all that separated me from the rocks below.

"What do you think you're bloody doing?" shouted the headmaster. "Slow down now!"

"I can't," I screamed. "Help!" The donkey bashed into the wall with such ferocity I had to dig my fingers deep into its neck to stop from plunging to my death. I overtook the other tourists and reached the plateau shaking with terror. About five men managed to finally stop the beast and helped me off its back. I had to sit down immediately to recover. A while later the headmaster reached the top. He walked up to me.

"Get up," he said. "You'd better make sure to come and see me when we get back on the ship. You are here as an ambassador to our school and I will not tolerate that sort of reckless behaviour."

When the other kids arrived he told us all that we had three hours to go off on our own to explore the island and not to be late getting back on the ship. I wandered round the market-place looking for trinkets. I was fascinated by the people. The way they dressed, talked and behaved was like nothing I had ever seen. The smells of roasting marinated meat made me slaver. I bought myself a wide brimmed straw hat and a kebab and walked over to some boys from my school that I spotted haggling with a stall owner over a flick-knife that he had for sale. One of them looked me up and down. Standing there in my school uniform with a straw hat and kebab grease saturating the front of my shirt I could appreciate the look of incredulity that appeared on his face.

"I'm not paying that!" Stig said to the stall owner. He turned to the other boys. "Fuck it, let's go. I spotted a bloke selling booze earlier. Let's give that a go."

We arrived at a stall where we watched as a customer filled a cola bottle with a clear liquid that came from the tap on a barrel.

I had first been made aware of alcohol at the tender age of nine. The fourteen year old son of a friend of my mother's introduced me to the delights of his dad's homebrew while all of the adults were in the living room. I remember walking into the living room with a nose bleed, telling everyone that I didn't feel very well. I just had time to register the shock on their faces before I passed out.

"How much is it for a bottle of that stuff, mate?" asked Luke. The stall owner told us that this was the finest ouzo in Greece and we could purchase it for the princely sum of the English equivalent of ten pence a bottle. Most of the boys took an instant dislike to the drink and those who did like it only drank in moderation.

"Does anybody want to bet that I can down a whole bottle of this in one go?" I asked the crowd.

"Fifty pence says you won't do it," said Stig.

"Done," I replied and promptly consumed the fiery liquid in one foul swoop as the other boys cheered me on. I put out my hand to Stig palm-up in expectation.

"Bollocks, I had my fingers crossed," he said and walked off with his cronies laughing. I felt the world start to spin.

"Are you alright?" asked Luke.

"No," I whispered pathetically and sat down on the ground.

"That was cool."

"Cheers." Tears started to roll down my face as my brain turned to mush and I began to panic, thinking that I was going to die. I looked up and noticed the stall owner calling his friends over and pointing to me while shaking his head in dismay.

"You're not looking too hot," Luke commented. "Maybe you should make yourself puke."

I leaned sideways and put my fingers down my throat. As soon as they touched my tonsils a stinking mixture of kebab and ouzo flew out of my mouth. I didn't react quickly enough and the vomit spattered my hand. I wiped it on my trousers as Luke helped me up.

"You won't tell anyone about this will you?" I pleaded in my stupor. I couldn't stand unassisted.

"I'm not going to need to," he said. "Look at the fucking state of you."

"I'll be alright in a few minutes." I wasn't.

Time was running out. We had twenty minutes to make it back to the ship and I was all over the place both mentally and physically.

"The headmaster's going to kill you," said Luke.

"Fuck him," I roared with drunken bravado. "I'll kick the old bastard's head in if he touches me."

Somehow I managed to avoid plummeting to my death on the way down the side of the volcano. Fortunately, I had been given a donkey with a more serene temperament. I noticed the headmaster glance in my direction, take a double-take and come marching over to me. I tried to get off the donkey but caught my foot in the stirrup as I swung my other leg across the animal's back to get off. I landed flat on my face with my left foot still in the stirrup. The hundred or so kids that witnessed the dismount cheered. I freed myself, sprang to my feet and took a bow.

"I thank you. I'll be here all week," I shouted to my audience. The headmaster looked at me with sheer hatred in his eyes.

"You're drunk!" he said.

"I'm not sir," I replied. "I think I had a kebab that didn't agree with me."

"We'll continue this conversation back on the ship. Now pull yourself together, you pathetic specimen." He returned to his wife and put his arm around her, steering her away from me.

Later, on board the ship when the headmaster decided to chastise me I realised, with relief, that the old bastard had forgotten to bring his strap with him. He still slapped me across the face and banned me from disembarking at the island of Rhodes as a punishment. I went back to the cabin and spent the rest of the day sleeping off my drunken stupor, having to get up regularly to dry-heave and cry in to the sink.

The next day there was a buzz of excitement. The kids chattered on about what they would do when they got to Rhodes that day. I was gutted. I spent the morning standing on the deck watching the trail of foam that the ship left in its wake as it ploughed majestically through the Mediterranean Sea.

"There's that twat who was pissed up, covered in puke," I heard somebody whisper to their friend. I was met with a lot of that sort of thing that morning; people, who would whisper to each other, giggle or stop talking when I approached. It just compounded the misery I was already feeling.

I decided to head back to the cabin. I turned and spotted a group of girls walking in my direction. The girl I had noticed the day we boarded the ship was there. As they walked past she glanced my way and smiled. My heart soared. I told Luke about it when back to the cabin.

"She was probably just trying not to laugh at you," he said.

"Bollocks. She fancies me," I insisted. Nothing he had to say about the encounter could dampen my spirits. She loved me. I knew it. I wasn't bothered anymore about everybody abandoning me for the day, I was in love and it was amazing. I spent the afternoon wandering up and down the ship, trying to figure out the best way to make my move. Luckily, Luke had his eye on her friend and he was far more gregarious and garrulous than me. I saw using him as the perfect opportunity.

Over the next few days the romance blossomed. Not mine of course, but Luke's. Due to her stature and the fact that her eyes were quite wide apart and protruded slightly Luke referred to her as Toady. Not the most affectionate term of endearment but it did suit her. I would spend hours on his shoulder like a spare part in the hope that her friend, Mandy, would speak to me. I had tried every cool stance I could think of. I put cream in my hair, wore my best clothes and even borrowed Luke's aftershave. Nothing seemed to work. There was no way I would try and talk to her. Every sentence that came to mind was just so corny. Everybody would be in hysterics if I tried that. No, I just had to wait it out, look good and eventually she would come to me. Luke seemed so gifted at it. Toady would gaze into his eyes and laugh at everything he said. He was supremely confident. I noticed that one of his tricks was to point at some passer-by and whisper some obviously derogatory comment in her ear and they would both burst into conspiratorial laughter. After two days of getting nowhere with my plan, I decided to give Luke's style a go. I just needed the right opportunity to present itself.

The next day we spent the morning in a market at the port of Alexandria before travelling on a knackered old bus down to Cairo where we were to visit the museum among other things. The heat on the bus was stifling so it was all the more welcoming when we were approached by kids selling bottles of pop as we got off the bus. Most of them had some kind of disability. Many of those were amputees. I noticed Mandy looking at the small boy that was offering her a bottle with some trepidation.

"Go on," I whispered in her ear. "He's 'armless." I nudged her nodding towards the boy's stump of a left arm and realising before she'd even looked at me that I'd well and truly fucked it.

"Get away from me you sicko," she looked at me in sheer disgust and walked off. She said something to her friends and they all turned and gave me the same look. I had been a fool. Not only had what I said been tasteless, it had also been corny and clichéd and that was what I had feared the most. I was a hopeless case.

Most of the kids were pretty impressed by the museum due to the fact that it housed corpses either entombed or mummified. We were all into dead bodies. The rest of the stuff in there we thought was boring.

After the museum we had a little walk around Cairo town centre. The headmaster pointed out the thousands of children begging. He said that begging was the only way they could make money to survive. He also said that many of the grown-ups would deliberately smash limbs or commit DIY amputations on their own children in order to give them a 'profession' where they could feed the whole family with the proceeds of their begging. You'd fucking love that job, I thought.

The next stop was Giza. The pyramids and Sphinx were every bit as awesome as I had expected them to be. It was late afternoon and from where I was standing I could see the sun touching the top of the biggest pyramid. I had my camera with me and walked around with Luke taking plenty of snaps. An authentically dressed Egyptian approached me asking if I would like him to take pictures of me sitting on his camel. The charge, he told me, was a pound. Not bad, in fact, very nice of him, I thought as I handed him my camera and climbed aboard his camel, my heart pounding with excitement. I was heads above everybody else on the camel's back, wearing an authentic Egyptian fez that I'd bought for a quid and holding a leather camel whip that had cost me the same. It didn't quite go with my school uniform and cheap sunglasses but I didn't care. As I took in the magnificent view from this elevated position I felt quite majestic. I glanced down and noticed the Egyptian was taking pictures of me with my camera as if his life depended on it. He stopped and looked at the camera quizzically. Great, I thought. He's used the whole bloody film and I haven't got another one. He pulled on the camel's harness and gestured for me to climb off. After I dismounted he put out his hand, holding the camera away from me with the other one. I fished out a pound note.

"No, five." He raised his hand to show five fingers. I was horrified. I only had five quid on me. I reluctantly handed him the five pounds. He returned my camera to me with a big shit-eating grin on his face. I put it in my rucksack. Bloody useless now, I thought. I walked back to the others, petulantly kicking sand as I went.

I spotted Luke in deep conversation with one of the many Egyptians.

"What's going on?" I asked him.

""This bloke reckons that if we follow him, he can take us through a hole in the fence to get some really good photographs of the Sphinx," he said enthusiastically.

"Don't bother," I replied. "My camera's out of film and besides, they're a bunch of thieving bastards." The Egyptian looked at me with mild hostility. I didn't think he fully understood what I said, but he got the gist. He turned to Luke and carried on with his hard sell.

"He only wants a quid for it," said Luke. "Come on, my mum and dad'll be really chuffed if I go back with some good snaps." I gave in. The Egyptian led us away from the crowd and through a hole in a fence. We were now walking down a long stretch of ground between the two front legs of the colossal Sphinx.

Suddenly, I was thrown against the wall and I felt the Egyptians hand around my throat.

"Money!" he demanded. I looked to Luke for assistance but he was sprinting away as fast as his lily-white little bastard legs could carry him. I swung my right arm and whipped the thief as hard as I could across the thigh with my camel whip. He yelped and let go. I legged it and eventually caught up with Luke as he merged with the crowd of tourists.

"Thanks a fucking lot!" I tried to shout at him, but it came out as a hoarse whisper. I was parched. I leant down and grabbed my knees to stop them shaking, trying to get my breath back. He offered me his can of pop.

"Sorry mate, I just shat myself when I saw him get you. I ran back to get help." He did seem genuinely sorry. I took a swig of his pop and, having got my breath back, decided to go back towards the bus. It was safer there. A few minutes later we noticed the same Egyptian that had tried to mug me approach the headmaster and his wife.

"Jesus, he's got some nerve," said Luke. "We'd better go and tell them not to go with him."

"Don't you dare," I said. "It'll serve the old bastard right if he gets his throat slit. And that stuck-up wife of his."

"Fair point," conceded Luke.

Five minutes later the Headmaster came out of the enclosure red-faced and shaking like a leaf. His wife followed in floods of tears. They walked up to a nearby armed policeman and I could see them gesticulating wildly in front of him. The policeman stood there with a smirk on his face, shrugging his shoulders and shaking his head. The head and his wife walked over to us.

"If anybody gets invited to go off with one of the locals for any reason whatsoever, you must refuse. Is that understood?" His wife was standing away from him averting her eyes.

"Yes sir," we all chanted. On the bus back to Alexandria there was excited speculation as to what the problem with the headmaster might have been. Luke and I kept quiet.

The next stop on the cruise was Turkey. The ship pulled in at the port of Dikili. We were reliably informed by the headmaster that we were near the island of Lesbos which was famous for its lesbians. I didn't know what a lesbian was but from the expressions of awe on the other boys' faces it was apparent that they did know. I kept my mouth shut so as not to look stupid. We all piled off and were given an hour to look around. The smells of the local food made my stomach rumble but the flies were really getting on my nerves; they didn't suffer from shyness. They were different to the flies I was used to back home. They weren't quite the size of bluebottles and they were light brown in colour. They kept landing on me and I was starting to lose the plot. I walked around batting at them and swearing. They were driving me mad. I noticed that the locals didn't seem at all bothered by them. They would occasionally bat one away lightly if it landed on their face but other than that they just let them crawl on them. I thought they were very tolerant.

We had been told that the kebabs were something to behold. As I walked around I noticed virtually everybody was eating one. I went up to the nearest vendor and joined the queue. The huge lump of meat on a rotating skewer was crawling with flies. The vendor was telling all of the concerned customers not to worry about the flies as they were very clean and ate any bacteria that was forming on the meat thus making it all the more healthy and flavoursome. Although they all seemed sceptical they invariably shrugged their shoulders and went ahead and bought some anyway. I got to the front of the queue and ordered my kebab, specifying that I didn't want any salad. A middle-aged English woman looked at me sternly.

"You should have the salad," she said. "It's good for you."

"Rabbits eat salad," I said. "They rarely live past the age of three. I think that tells you something." She gave me a dirty look and walked off. The kebab was delicious.

After an hour's wandering we were all herded back together and taken to a mosque. I wasn't keen on having to take my shoes off as we entered but I did enjoy the experience of watching the people chanting their prayers. The rituals seemed so alien to the religious experiences I had had. As we left some of the kids were ridiculing the locals by imitating their chants. I kept my distance for fear of being tarred with the same brush by the teacher that was writing their names in his notebook.

Before returning to the ship we were taken to some old ruins where the guide told us all about the Ottoman Empire. I stopped listening after a while as I noticed many of the kids and teachers seemed to be disappearing. Luke tapped me on the shoulder. He was bent over holding his stomach.

"Help me get back to the ship," he groaned. "I think I'm going to shit myself." I grabbed his arm and escorted him back towards the port. As we got closer I noticed that most of the passengers were trying to push their way to the front of the queue back on to the ship. Most of them were holding on to their stomachs too. Some of them had wet brown stains down the back of their trousers and skirts. Luke suddenly stopped and grabbed my arm hard. A wet farty sound came from his behind. He started crying.

"Oh God help me," he moaned. "Quick, get me on the ship, I've shat myself. He had. It stunk. I gagged.

"I can't mate. The smell's making me feel sick." I let go of his arm.

"Don't leave me," he sobbed.

"Sorry Luke. I can't do it," I said and walked back into the town to wait for the queue to die down. There was no way I was going to stand in line with that lot. As I walked away I noticed the woman who had chastised me for not having the salad. She was lying on a bench on her side, clutching her stomach and crying. That'll teach you, I thought. The whole experience did nothing to cure my aversion to greens.

A while later it was safe to board the ship. The stench that hit me made my eyes water. There was a queue of hundreds waiting to see the ship's doctor. I returned to the cabin. The only people there when I returned were the

Germans. They seemed to be the only people other than myself who hadn't been poisoned. One of them had a guitar. I merrily spent the rest of the afternoon letting him teach me how to play a popular guitar riff while the rest of the passengers shat and cried.

For the rest of the cruise I kept myself to myself. I had lost faith in Luke as a friend after his spectacular display of cowardice. He didn't seem too keen on my company either after I had left him stewing in his own shit on the gangplank. The potential romance with Mandy had died a death; any glances she cast my way were scornful at best. I gave up trying to woo her even though I couldn't stop thinking about what might have been. I had no choice but to stay with the group whenever we disembarked but the rest of the time I spent hanging over the back of the ship, occasionally being hit with fleeting desires to jump. There was no real suicidal intent in these feelings, just a longing to recapture the emotions I had had in the past when the power of the sea brought me to life. I really had enjoyed the experience as a whole but the thought of returning to school always succeeded in dampening my spirits.

As we left the ship behind and got on the bus that was to take us back to school I caught a glimpse of Mandy sitting by the window of her bus. Our eyes met and she immediately turned away to talk to her friend, leaving me with an aching heart and dreams of a life that I was never going to live.

Chapter 27

Halfway through every term we had 'Visiting Day.' This was always on a Sunday. One of the many brilliant things about it was that we didn't have to go to church. When I was interviewed for my place at the school the headmaster asked me what denomination I was. I had been christened catholic, but I asked him why he needed to know. As my mother was present he overlooked this act of insolence and told me that Catholics had to go to church every Sunday while Church of England went every fortnight. As neither my mother nor I were particularly religious I knew I would get away with telling him that I was of the latter persuasion. This wily decision backfired as he told me that on the Sundays when we did not go to church we were visited by the local Young Christians. I had previous experience of Happy Clappers and did not relish the prospect of having to put up with these people twice a month for the next five years.

"Actually..." I began. My mother nudged me sharply in the ribs.

"Yes?"

"Nothing." Bugger!

On visiting days I was usually visited my mother who would bring along supplies for my tuck box. She would board the coach in the city and take the two hour journey to see me. We would usually walk the two miles across hills and glens in to the local village and have lunch in a café. I had to be careful where I took her; there were more than a couple of shopkeepers who had their eye on me, waiting to catch me in the act of pinching some trinket or other. I had so far eluded them.

There was one fat beady-eyed little bastard who really

had it in for the boarding school kids. I was asked to keep a look out one day as one of the boys decided to try and steal a build-it-yourself model of a battleship. Unfortunately the dimensions of the box were about two feet by eighteen inches, but this didn't deter the boy from trying to stuff it up his jumper. I cringed and watched in horror as the shopkeeper - who had been practically hanging off the boy, waiting for him to make his move – pounced. He grabbed the boy by the hair and dragged him towards the back of the shop.

"You!" he shouted pointing a podgy finger in my direction. "Come here now. I'm calling the Police!" I scarpered. When I arrived back at school it turned out that the boy had informed both the police and the headmaster of my involvement in the crime. I denied it until I was blue in the face but to no avail. The police had left it up to the headmaster to determine our fate. Our punishment consisted of the usual six of the strap, detention for a week and a thousand 'lines' – 'I will not bring the school into disrepute.'

There was one visiting day when my mum couldn't make it. I was informed by letter that my paternal grandparents would be coming in her stead. I was mortified; not only would they undoubtedly bring me the wrong tuck for my tuck box, but they would also bring my uncle Philip.

Unfortunately, the joy I felt at the prospect of being reunited with my grandparents on visiting day was tainted by the fact that my peers would annihilate me when they saw me in the company of Philip. I could not allow this to happen.

When visiting day arrived I ran down the school drive to the main road an hour before they were due to arrive.

There was one other kid already there waiting. I only hoped his family would arrive first so that he wouldn't witness the company I would be keeping. I had no doubt that he had his reasons for being there so early. It was obvious by the way he ignored me and nervously paced up and down the drive. The trouble was, whoever's family arrived first would be the only one to suffer. No-one could keep their mouth shut in that place, especially not me. After half an hour of waiting we both stood stock still and just stared down the road at the oncoming traffic, each of us praying that the other's family would arrive first.

My heart sank as the familiar sight of my grandfather's car came around the bend towards us. They pulled up beside me and my grandmother wound down her window. We exchanged greetings.

"What are you doing out here? She asked. "You're mum said we were to meet you in the car-park."

"Err, yeah. Well, it's a nice day. I thought we could all go into the village and have lunch?"

"Aren't you going to show us where you're staying?" she asked. "We'd love a tour of the school."

"Can't we just go to the village?" I asked. It seemed that realization was dawning. The saddened expression on her face told me everything. I guiltily climbed into the back of the car and sat by Philip who put his arm around me. I looked out of the window and saw the other kid watching me as we drove off. He was smirking. I glared at him. I will fucking kill you, I thought.

Chapter 28

The next day Mr McEwan, knowing I was a bit of a horror buff and had done particularly well in the spelling test that week, invited me to watch the late night horror film in his flat as a reward.

"Can I bring my mate?" I asked, desperately searching my mind for somebody I could ask. I was only too aware of the rumours circulating about some of the teachers but I was confident that this man wasn't one of them. He wasn't a monster; he was about the only thing that kept me going in that place. But you couldn't be too careful.

"Well, I don't see why not," he replied. "I'll come and give you a nudge at about half past ten."

I was lying in bed awake, having failed in my mission to find someone to accompany me. I glanced to my left and noticed Slash was still awake. No, I thought, I'll never live it down if somebody sees me leave the dormitory with him. They'll think I've pissed the bed too.

It was twenty past ten. Sod it! I looked left again, he was still awake. I leant across and nudged him.

"No, I haven't pissed yet, leave me alone!" he spat.

"I wasn't going to ask you that," I said. "Although it's just as well 'cause I was going to ask you if you wanted to come and watch a horror film in McEwan's flat. I've been invited," I said proudly.

"Ok," he replied. "Sorry about biting your head off, I just get a bit touchy about that. I can't help it you know. It's a medical condition. Anyway, what're you asking me for? Scared he'll bum you if you go on your own?"

"No," I lied." I just felt guilty for taking the pi... I mean mickey out of you. Now get your slippers on, he'll be here in a minute."

A short while later he came into the dorm, saw we were awake, put his finger to his lips and beckoned us to follow.

His flat was located at the opposite end of the dormitory to the housemaster's. It was tiny, but a damn sight bigger than the bed space that I had to call home for five years. It was cluttered with cricket memorabilia. Ornaments, pictures and old bats left next to no space to sit, plus the fact that there was only room for one armchair. Though we had to sit on the floor in front of the black and white portable TV we were made to feel more than welcome with offers of squash and rich tea biscuits which I suspected had been swiped from the servery.

He turned off the big light and put the film on before sitting in his armchair behind us. After my initial trepidation I was soon lost in the mood of the old Dracula film we were watching. When the film finished the television station closed down to the sound of the National Anthem. Mr McEwan insisted we stand to attention for the duration of the music. We were then sent back to our dormitory. As I climbed into bed I noticed one of the other boys leering at me. That's all I need, I thought.

As I lay there trying to go to sleep I reassessed my feelings about the school. Maybe the other kids were erroneous in their beliefs that the teachers harboured nothing but impure thoughts towards the boys. Don't get me wrong, I was only too aware of the sadistic nature of many of them, but I was beginning to doubt they could be capable of anything more sinister. After all, ostensibly I had just done exactly the same as the boy who had gone to the housemaster's flat in the dead of night. And I was ok.

Chapter 29

The next morning I returned from breakfast to get ready for inspection. As I walked through the lobby and looked towards my bed I noticed something scrawled across my headboard in felt tip. Great, I thought, what is it going to say? Teacher's bum boy, pissy pal, something like that. As I got closer and was able to make out the words my blood began to boil. Across the headboard was daubed the legend 'MONG LOVER.' I looked around but couldn't see the kid from visiting day. I ran out of the dormitory heading for the dining room.

As I walked in there the heads of the stragglers that remained in the hall all turned to me. The teacher stood and called me to his table. I ignored the summons and scanned the room looking for the culprit. I spotted him walking away from me with his breakfast tray in his hands. I ran at him full pelt and knocked him onto the floor. His tray went flying across the hall, the crockery shattering as it hit the floor. As I kicked him repeatedly in the side of the head I noticed there was no sign of shock on his face as he checked out his assailant. I knew I had the right person. I was suddenly smashed into the wall. All of the air was knocked out of me and I struggled for breath as I felt the sharp stinging agony of bamboo rain down repeatedly about my head and upper body. I curled myself into a ball until the attack ended.

"Get up," said the teacher. "If you don't get suspended for this I'll be very surprised," he said as he dragged me out of the dining room and made me stand against the outside wall. The fight in me had gone, I was drained. The prospect of being suspended horrified me. Much as I relished the thought of going home, the disappointment my mother would feel would kill me. I didn't want to let her down.

"Sorry sir," I said pitifully as tears began to roll down my cheeks

"What was that all about?" he asked. He seemed genuinely concerned.

"Nothing, sir. It was inexcusable."

Although I felt nothing but hatred towards the other boy, there was no way I was going to grass. I had seen what happened to such boys. The other pupils ostracised and bullied them and the teachers never stuck up for them. They had also been conditioned into the belief reporting of wrongdoing was the bolt hole of the cretin who could not fight his own battles.

"Go and clean yourself up," he sighed. I walked away in the direction of the ablution block.

When I returned to the dormitory to prepare for the inspection all of the pupils in the dorm were making stupid noises and faces at me, sticking their tongues under their bottom lips and simulating sex moves. I ignored them and set about scrubbing the graffiti off my headboard with a nailbrush.

I wasn't really in the mood for schoolwork that day and subsequently spent an hour in detention after school writing lines about how I must pay more attention in class.

After tea I had an hour and a half free time before prep. I couldn't face the taunts anymore and I was too tired to fight so I just went and sat by the woods at the bottom of the football field. I could se the woodwork teacher's children playing in their garden, throwing a Frisbee to each other until their mother called them in. I longed to go home and go to a normal school. I'd had enough of this place. Even Joe and Luke were taking the piss.

That night in bed I reached into my drawer and found my knife. Even though I had contemplated taking my own life with it before, this time I was determined to do it. I got my torch and a pen and paper and wrote a suicide note. It wasn't exactly 'Goodbye cruel world' but it wasn't a million miles away. I put the note on top of my bedside cabinet where I was sure it would be found and pressed the tip of the knife against my sternum. I pushed the knife until I felt the skin give and I became aware of a small pool of blood welling in the dent the knife had made. I stopped for a minute. I tried to search my mind for a reason not to do it. All I could think of was the fact that we had chips for tea the next day. I loved chips. Would they have chips in heaven? I wondered. Probably not. I carefully came to the conclusion that this was as good a reason as any to carry on living so I put the knife back in the drawer, screwed up my note and went to sleep.

Chapter 30

It was Tuesday. As was often the case I was to read out this morning's bible reading to the school. I was in one of my dark moods.

I often felt angry, wanting to hit hard at everybody who came near me. I was furious at the fact that I was alone with no-one to tell me that I was worth a fuck or needed. Well, bollocks to you all, I thought. I was damned if I was going to tell everybody how lucky we all were. I didn't feel lucky; I felt betrayed and abandoned. I was still being derided for being stupid enough to be related to somebody who was mentally handicapped. That morning I'd walked to breakfast enduring calls of 'Spaz shagger' and having kids walk in front of me mimicking the mentally and physically handicapped. I'd had enough.

I was called up to do my bit. I walked dutifully up to the lectern, looked down as if to start my reading, kicked the pulpit to the floor as hard as I could and legged it out of there. I ran to the bottom of the football pitch and charged into the forest, cutting my hands as I forced the sharp branches out of the way. I ran for what felt like hours until sheer exhaustion drove me to my knees. I sat there waiting to get my breath back. For a fifteen year old I knew I was in good shape and was sharp enough to elude my pursuers. I burst out laughing like a lunatic. I was elated. I was spitting bloody feathers, I needed water. If I had used my bloody head I would have waited until nightfall when I could have gathered some essentials, changed into less conspicuous clothing and slipped out unnoticed. Still, spilt milk and all that.

I trundled on until I found a stream. I plunged my head into it and drank. I was unconcerned about getting a stomach bug from eating or drinking anything in the woods. While I was living in Brighton with my grandmother I contracted salmonella. My grandmother was scatterbrained and rarely cooked; when she did it was abysmal. She swore blind that I'd caught it from a dodgy hot-dog on the sea front, but I knew better. I started getting severe stomach cramps during class one day and put up my hand to ask permission to go to the toilet. I was chastised severely for not going before the lesson; however the teacher let me go. I sat down on the toilet and passed out. They had to break down the toilet door and grab me, pants around my ankles and all, and got an ambulance to take me to hospital. Suspecting meningitis, they then gave me a lumbar puncture which crippled me. After the correct diagnosis of salmonella they began to question me about my lifestyle. When they found out that my grandmother was usually at work after school and that I had to climb through a window to get in they called her in and offered her some stern advice. It wasn't something that bothered me at all but they didn't seem too chuffed about it. The long and short of it is that this illness made me indestructible. I was never again to be plagued by stomach bugs. This was one of the few attributes I possessed that made me feel pretty special. I would fantasise about an apocalypse, living in a world where there would only be me and the cockroaches and I could live like a king. I would live in Buckingham Palace and live on crisps and chocolate that my mutated insectile servants would bring from the shops.

    After replenishing myself from the stream I took stock of my surroundings and tried to get my bearings. I knew that my home town was about sixty miles south of the school and I pretty much knew all of the roads that would take me there. I just had to find my way out of the woods and find the road. I knew the sun rose in the east. It was still morning and the sun was on my right; I was heading in the right direction towards home. By my reckoning I needed to head east to find the main road. I set off. I was on a roll. I had the whole day ahead of me to find my way out of the forest and I had spotted a source of sustenance. It was the beginning of October and there were blackberries everywhere. I wasn't going to starve.

It had clouded over and was getting cold and dark. I still hadn't found my way out of the woods. I could no longer rely on the position of the sun to guide me and concluded that I was well and truly lost. I carried on traipsing, all the while listening out for the sound of passing cars. All I could hear was the rustling of the wind in the trees. After eating about a hundred blackberries already, I had concluded that I never wanted to see another one again and was starting to get a bit worried about where my next meal would come from. I sat against a tree to rest.

I opened my eyes and realised that I had fallen asleep. The forest was pitch black and it was pouring with rain. So far nothing was going according to plan. I had expected to be out of the forest hours ago and well on my way home. Best laid plans! I stood and tried to shake the pins and needles out of my legs, noticing that I was soaked to the skin and freezing cold. I suddenly heard the loud continuous sound of something crashing through the woods to my left. I knew it wasn't a werewolf, there was no such thing, besides the moon wasn't visible due o the storm clouds overhead. Still, there might actually be a full moon above them. Did it work like that? I didn't know, but I wasn't going to take any chances. I began to run blindly through the forest, away from what I was convinced was pursuing me. I had gone about twenty yards when I slipped and went flying down a muddy hill on my back. I hit a tree and lay there out of breath trying to listen for the sound of what was not a werewolf coming to rip my throat out. All I could hear was the deafening sound of the rain hitting the leaves of the canopy above my head.

I was scared and starting to regret my decision. I should have planned it more carefully. I resolved to find my way out of the woods and face the music. I stood and carried on wandering blindly for hours until I eventually found the road. I could just see a glimmer of daylight on the horizon. I guessed it to be about four a.m. It seemed like I'd lost what was not a werewolf. I hadn't heard any funny noises for the rest of my struggle through the forest. I turned right began heading back in the direction of the school. I estimated a four mile walk. As it started to get lighter I was able to see the state I was in. I was still soaking wet and my uniform was totally brown with mud. My normally gleaming black shoes were ruined. I sat down in a puddle and watched a crow that was gnawing away at a dead rabbit in the middle of the road. I welcomed the company. My thoughts turned back to school and I was beginning to wonder how I would get my uniform clean when I heard a car coming up from the direction of the village. I turned and sighed as I realised it was the police. The crow flew away and I stood up.

The policeman got out of his car, went to the boot and took out a large picnic blanket which he covered the back seat with.

"Get in," he said despairingly. I climbed in. He muttered something into his radio. We didn't exchange words on the drive back to school. I guessed he'd seen it all before.

As we arrived at the gates we were greeted by Mr

McEwan who must have been on duty that night. The policeman got out and spoke to him for a minute before the teacher came to the car and opened the door.

"Come on lad," he said quietly. "Let's get you cleaned up and fed, shall we." I was gobsmacked. I was expecting the hiding of my life. I knew that some of the other teachers would have gone to town on my backside with their sticks and slippers. He escorted me to the ablution block, stopping off at the laundry room on the way to get me some clean towels. On his advice I went into the hot shower fully clothed to wash the worst of the mud off and then he told me to strip off my clothes to clean my body. He threw me a sachet of body shampoo and told me to pass him my dirty clothes.

"I'll take these down to the laundry while you sort yourself out. Back in five minutes." He left carrying my dripping uniform in his outstretched arms. I came out of the shower and wrapped a towel around my bottom half. I started to wipe my shoes clean and looked up at the clock. It was five thirty a.m. The other boys would be woken up in an hour and a half.

Mr McEwan came back in and passed me a pair of slippers that turned out to be a couple of sizes too small.

"Follow me," he said and led me outside. The sun had risen but the cold of the October morning still froze me to the core. He led me back to his flat at the end of the dormitory. He invited me to sit down in his armchair and offered me a blanket while he fired up the portable gas heater. I was given a cup of tea and two slices of toast. It was cheap margarine but I wasn't going to complain. I wolfed it down.

"I don't want to put you in an awkward position by making you tell me what all this was about and who was responsible, he said. " I've got a pretty good idea. We see and hear a lot more than you might think. You have to stop worrying what others think of you. Be your own man. You know a lot more about what's right and wrong than any of that lot. You're special, regardless of what you believe anybody else thinks. You can't be offended by people whose opinion you don't respect. Let it go and leave this school with a bit of bloody self respect lad." He put his arm around me and gave my shoulder a reassuring squeeze.

"You'd best go and get yourself into bed," he said. "You're only going to be getting about an hour's sleep as it is. But listen. As far as everybody else is concerned, even your best mates, I've given you a bloody good thrashing, ok?"

"Yes sir," I replied.

"Be on your way then." I left, still feeling quite numb and in a state of bewilderment.

Chapter 31

I went to bed and lay there wide awake until we were ordered to rise by the housemaster. I was grateful that I had a sympathetic shoulder to cry on but I was more concerned about whether the mockery from the other boys would escalate. I had to find a way to divert their attention away from me or do something they would admire. It turned out that I didn't have too much to worry about; the fact that I had beaten the life out of my tormenter and then done a bunk seemed to have redeemed me in their eyes. Everybody secretly wanted to escape but few had the guts to try it.

"Nice one Stonekicker," somebody called across to me. "You had the teachers shitting themselves."

I looked down the aisle at the boy who had started all this. He was sporting a nice black eye and a hangdog expression on his face.

"Hey McDonut, bet you'll think twice about crossing Stonekicker again, won't you?" said Luke.

"Fuck off," the boy replied.

"Hey Stonekicker, smack his arse again, he's getting lippy," somebody else said. I was very tired but felt a huge amount of relief at the way this had panned out. I was glad they were making him suffer and I intended to make life much worse for him from now on. I walked up to him.

"Have you got anything to say to me?" I asked him.

"Soz," he replied. It wasn't the most heartfelt apology I had ever heard but it was something. I head-butted him in the face. He fell down on the bed with a bleeding nose.

"Twat," I said and walked off to breakfast.

As I walked into the dining hall I was greeted with a cheer from the rest of the pupils. I sat down at the head of my table and took a bowl of cereal from one of the younger boys who glared at me with indignation.

"Problem?" I asked him.

"No."

"Thought not," I said and dug into my breakfast. Being a fifth year table-head really did have its perks.

My fellow table-head was Bonehead.

"I wouldn't stand for that kind of behaviour," he said to me. "He's taking the piss out of you. I think he needs the salt-pot."

"Nah, he's alright," I replied.

"He fucking isn't," snarled Bonehead. "Oy, Put your hand out," he said to the boy. The younger boys were terrified of him and were too scared to answer back. The boy dutifully put out his hand with tears already welling in his eyes.

I leant close to Bonehead's ear and whispered to him. "I said he was alright."

"And I said he fucking isn't." He picked up the salt pot and sprinkled some salt on the back of the boy's hand in order to intensify the pain when he delivered the blow. He raised his hand and was just about to do it when I turned and landed an upper-cut under his chin. He flew backwards in his chair and landed in a heap on the floor.

"What the hell's going on over there?" shouted the teacher.

"He leaned backwards and fell, sir," I called back. "Didn't you?" I said to Bonehead.

"Yes sir. It was an accident sir. Sorry sir."

"Well I hope that taught you a lesson," said the teacher who immediately lost interest and tucked back into his porridge. Bonehead climbed back into his chair with blood coming out of his mouth from having bitten his tongue.

"Thanks," said the boy whose hand I had saved.

"Here you go," I said and handed the boy Bonehead's bowl of cereal. "I think he's lost his appetite."

I knew to expect some violent repercussions from my act of chivalry. I had broken the unwritten rule of not taking sides with a fellow fifth year against a younger pupil. Word travel fast and I might need to dodge a few uppercuts myself. I really wasn't bothered by this though. I only wished I had had the courage not to go with the crowd years ago. I had often had a bit of a rebellious streak against the authorities but I had always been terrified of looking bad in front of my peers. I felt a sudden sense of release from these bonds that had tied me for so long. It was euphoric. I believed I had finally developed the tools to be my own person and be strong enough to deal with whatever the world threw at me. For the first time in my life I thought that I was actually worth something. These rare good deeds I performed did make me get a bit carried away with myself, I must admit. I was sure it wouldn't be long before some bugger knocked me back down to size. I came up with a plan. I knew exactly which of the bastards would jump at the chance to knock me down after what I had just done. It was simple. I just had to get them before they got me. If all went well it may even improve my current status as seventh hardest in the school. Now that would be cool.

Throughout the day I noticed the other kids repeatedly
When lunc
dining hall
without a word. The smaller kids at the table kept nervously glancing up at us but nobody said anything. Ther was rather an unpleasant atmosphere to say the least.

That afternoon after the last class of the day had

finished, Luke approached me.

"Thought I'd give you the heads-up," he said. "I've heard that Clock is going to do you later."

"Thought he might," I replied. Clock, as well as being the toughest, was also the nastiest kid in the school. He had his own rules and regulations that we were all supposed to abide by. Maintaining a united front in front of the younger boys was one of them.

"What the fuck did you go and do that for? In front of the bloody sprogs as well. Have you got a death wish? I mean, you could have waited until you were back in the dorm."

"I couldn't care less," I said. "He had it coming."

Luke shook his head and walked off.

About half an hour before we were due to start prep, I walked into the canteen. There were a few fifth years hanging around the pool table but most of the kids were in the TV room watching a music programme. I spotted Clock throwing a younger boy out of a chair at the front. The boy sulkily got up and went to sit at the back so that Clock could have the best seat. I looked around for a weapon. All I could find was a wooden skittle from the skittle alley. I picked it up and assessed its suitability. It would have to do. Although I was tall for my age I didn't measure up against Clock. He was only sixteen years old but he was six feet two inches tall and very well built. I needed to be fast. I squeezed my way through the chairs and came up behind him. Some of the other kids were asking me to get out of the way but Clock hadn't turned around yet. So far, so good. I pulled my arm back and swung the skittle towards his overly large head. It hit him on his right ear and knocked him off his seat. He fell to the floor clutching his ear screaming.

"I hear you wanted a word with me," I said to him calmly. He tried to get to his feet but I kicked him in the throat and put him back down. I dropped the skittle and turned to leave. Four of Clock's cronies blocked my exit. Two of them were the Fat Ginger Bullies. They all carried pool cues. I didn't have a hope. Bugger. I looked behind me and Clock was getting to his feet. They all charged me at once. I'd had it. I felt a pool cue jab me in the left cheek and I dropped to the floor and curled myself into a defensive ball. The blows rained down on me. I couldn't make out what they were shouting but when they were done Clock bent down and spat in my face.

"You are a fucking dead man," he said as they dropped their weapons and left the building. As I struggled to get to my feet I thought that I really should have checked who else was in there before I attacked him. I tried to figure out where this all left me. One of his cronies was only ranked twelfth hardest in the year. The Fat Ginger Bullies were joint fourth. As the one who was twelfth place had just been instrumental in my beating, did that put me at thirteenth now? I wasn't sure if a group beating counted. I suppose it did. If I had succeeded in my plan then I guessed that would have put me on the top. It was all very confusing. I thought I'd better put it all behind me and concentrate on how I was going to survive the rest of the term. I had the feeling I was going to need eyes in the back of my head. As I staggered towards the dorm I noticed that my bloody rib had gone again. Great!

Chapter 32

There was a boy in the dormitory who had to be on a par with me when it came to the amount of times he had been punished, but where my punishments were invariably a result of my being just plain stupid his were a result of never being able to maintain a tidy bed space or appearance, hence the nickname 'Rubbish'. What I found most ironic and admirable was the fact that he was a bigger stonekicker than me and didn't care one iota what people thought of him. I would like to have got to have known him better if it weren't for the fact that I still found it a necessity to keep the crowd happy. It didn't take long to realise that my decision to maintain this façade was indeed the right one.

During the five years I spent at the school I had only known of one boy being suspended. Nobody had been expelled. The fact that there was a large proportion of boys who had come to our school having already been expelled meant that there was nowhere else for them to go since the dissolution of the Borstals. Besides, the teachers knew that that was what most of us wanted. We didn't care about our futures; we just wanted to get out of the bloody place. Expulsion would have been playing right into our hands. Although it gave the teachers the power to inflict whatever punishments they chose on us, this unwritten rule did, however, give carte blanche to those buggers intent on pushing the boundaries.

One Sunday afternoon while I was laying on my bed reading, Joe came running into the dorm.

"Hey Stonekicker, you've got to come and see this."
"What?"
"Just follow me."

I followed him out of the dorm and down to the drying room. This was where we hung our washed clothes to dry. It was a small room with blistering hot pipes around the walls and no windows. As we entered the room I saw Luke standing there with a rugby sock in his hand that had a wooden nail brush stuffed inside. I then noticed Rubbish tied to a chair in the middle of the room, crying.

"What's going on?" I asked.

"Watch this," said Luke.

"Are you bent," Joe asked the boy sitting in the chair.

"No," whimpered Rubbish.

"Wrong answer. Lights," he nodded to Luke who dutifully turned off the light. It became pitch black. I heard the sound of wood hitting bone, followed by a piercing howl. The light came back on.

"Untie me now!" shouted Rubbish, his eyes streaming.

"Try again, shall we?" asked Joe. He looked at me. "Do you want to have a pop at him this time?" he asked me. I didn't.

"Er, go on then," I replied. He handed me the sock and turned back to Skid.

"Are you bent?" he repeated.

"NO!"

He turned off the light and I swung the sock down hard. I was rewarded with a squeal. The light came back on. I avoided making eye contact with anybody. The torture continued until eventually Rubbish succumbed to the demands and told us that yes, in fact, he was bent. Joe untied him and we left.

I left the other two and walked down to the hedge at the bottom of the field to see if there were any animals I could watch. I looked across the field at the hills in the distance. The clouds were covering the top of them and there was a fine drizzle coming down. After two minutes in this I was soaking wet. I sat down on the grass by the hedge and looked longingly into the wood beyond.

I wished I had the guts to have stopped the boys from hurting Rubbish. I had felt scared when I saw what they were doing, but a part of me that I did not want to acknowledge felt exhilarated at the power I felt as I wielded the rugby sock and hit him with it. This disturbed me the most, the fact that I might be getting a taste for this sadistic behaviour. I realised that the fear I had felt was not fear of hurting Rubbish and causing him distress, more the fear of being caught in the act. I had to find a way of turning this around. Find a way of avoiding these situations and clawing back some self respect. I thought about what my parents would have to say about what I had done. I didn't doubt for a second that my dad would be impressed. He would believe that I was becoming a man and would be proud of the fact that I was looking after myself. My mother, on the other hand, would be deeply distressed by my actions. She had always tried to instil in me her sense of decency and respect for everybody else. I could never confess my sins to her.

I took a biscuit from my pocket, put it under the hedge and waited until a field mouse eventually turned up to nibble at it. I stayed there until I heard the bell ring for tea then squelched my way back to the dining hall.

Chapter 33

The three of us were in the village one Saturday afternoon when Luke suggested that we all get stoned.

"How are we going to do that?" I asked. It wasn't like the city I lived in where there were certain areas you could go and buy dope from; this was a small village where the only crimes were those committed by the kids at the boarding school up the road, and these were only things like stealing and fighting. Besides, we were only kids and even if there was somewhere to buy dope from they probably wouldn't sell it to us. We only had forty pence a week pocket money.

"Lighter gas!" said Luke.

Ten minutes later we were sitting on a fence in a field on the way back to school. Luke had the canister in his hand.

"Here you go," he said. "You give it a try." He offered me the can.

"I ain't doing it," I said. "That stuff could probably kill you." I'd frequently smuggled test-tubes filled with pure alcohol from the chemistry lab and had become quite partial the stuff, but lighter fuel was something else.

"Puff," he replied and offered it to Joe.

"How do you do it?" he asked.

"Grip the nozzle hard with your teeth and push it down. Look, watch." We heard a loud hiss as the gas went into his mouth. He did this three times.

"Fucking hell, it works!" he said. "I'm stoned. Come on, have a go." He offered me the can again. I declined. He shook his head in dismay as Joe also refused to participate.

"You two don't know what you're missing, "he said in a slurred voice then promptly threw up down his shirt and fell off the fence. Joe and I tried to pick him up, but he just lay there crying, saying how ill he felt. We thought we'd better leave him for a bit.

We both sat down on the grass and Joe got his cigarettes out of his pocket and offered me one.

As I lit up Joe said, "Keep that match away from Luke, his head'll explode with all that gas he's been inhaling." We sat there smoking and laughing and making sure Luke stayed lying on his side to stop him from choking on his own puke.

After Luke had sufficiently recovered we headed back to school. As we entered the dormitory I noticed Clock and the Ginger Bullies watching me malevolently. Luke and Joe made themselves scarce, leaving me on my own. I'd remember that. Clock made a pathetic imitation of cutting his throat with his finger while looking at me. I wasn't intimidated but I wished they would just get it over and done with. I found the anticipation of a beating was worse than the beating itself. I had tried to come up with a plan to get them before they got me but in the end I realised that it was pointless. It wouldn't make things any better; it would just start a war that could get out of hand. I didn't really fancy my chances against any of them in a fair fight either. Besides, I would just be stooping to their level. I'd already done a lot of things that I wasn't proud of but I was damned if I was going to do any more. I'd spent most of the last five years pretending to be something I wasn't. I decided to give Clock his moment of glory. At least I would be able to rest again without constantly looking over my shoulder or waiting behind after class for everybody to go before I left. I couldn't be arsed with all that malarkey any more. It would be slightly suicidal of me but hey, fuck it.

"Sorry, Clock," I said (nobody had ever called him

that to his face before). "Did I interrupt your bumming session with that pair of ginger retards?" That did the trick.

After I had endured one of the biggest kick-ins of my life my situation seemed to improve dramatically. Sure, I got the odd dirty look off them, but I could see that they all felt that justice had been served and they all decided to move on to somebody else. Luke.

A couple of days later I spotted the three of them dragging a sleeping bag that obviously had a body in it across to the ablution block. I could hear screaming coming from inside the bag. I watched with anticipation as they entered the block. Two minutes later they all came running out, laughing. They had the empty sleeping bag with them. I waited until they were out of sight and walked into the block to see what was going on. I could hear the showers were on. It was six o'clock on a Friday. Nobody should have been in there. Luke came out of the showers shivering and covered in bruises.

"What happened?" I asked.

"I was reading a magazine on my bed when the fuckers pounced on me." It was hard to tell exactly what he was saying as his teeth were chattering and every word was followed by a loud sniff. "They stripped my clothes off, ripping half of them in the process, shoved me in the sleeping bag, punched the crap out of me and threw me in the cold shower. Now I'm stuck here bollock naked.

"Why did they do it? Was it a porno you were reading?"

"Yeah."

"Well, there you go then," I said.

"Will you go over to the dorm and get me some clothes to wear otherwise I'll have to walk all the way back in the nuddy?"

"I'm not being funny mate, but I don't seem to recall you coming to my rescue in the past," I said. "In fact, you did the bloody opposite. Every time I've had a problem you've legged it, so as far as I'm concerned you can ram it. Besides, they'll know it was me that helped you, and I don't want to get into all that shit with them again." I walked out of the block leaving Luke hurling a torrent of abuse at me. It was about time somebody else did a bit of suffering.

I got back to the dorm and looked out of the window, waiting to see what he would do. After a few minutes I was rewarded with the sight of him running as fast as he could back to the dorm with both of his hands covering his bits. The Art teacher drove past in his little sports car. He didn't stop to see what the problem was but I did notice him shaking his head despairingly.

Luke tried to get his own back on me later that evening. I was lying on my bed with a book when I spotted him come into the dormitory carrying a bottle of pop. He saw me and went behind the wall that separated the two halves of the dormitory. He obviously believed that I couldn't see him from my vantage point. This was true, but I could see everything he was doing from the reflection in the mirror that was on the wall at the far end of the dorm. I watched as he took the lid off his bottle and urinated in it. He put the lid back on and walked in the dorm as if nothing had happened.

"Sorry about shouting at you earlier," he said. "I was just pissed off after what had happened and took it out on you. I can see where you're coming from. Come on, let's have a drink and let bygones be bygones." He offered me the bottle.

"Nah, you're alright," I said.

"Come on, have a drink on me," he persisted.

"I'm not into drinking other peoples piss, so I won't bother." His face blanched.

"What are you talking about? It's just shandy." he said.

"I know you've pissed in it," I said.

"Look," he said. "It's fine." He took a large swig from the bottle and swallowed. "See?" My stomach turned.

"I watched you do it. I could see you in the mirror that's down the end of the dorm," I said.

"Oh," he whispered painfully. "I think I'm going to be sick." He ran out of the dorm. I wasn't that experienced when it came down to how friends should treat each other but I did have a suspicion that our 'friendship' was well and truly over. Honestly! I thought. You don't try and make your mates drink your piss. It's just not something friends do. It appeared that I was on my own again. That suited me just fine.

Chapter 34

My belief that I was better off without these friends was reinforced later that term. It was about two o'clock in the morning when I awoke and noticed Luke and Joe leave the dormitory.

Although things had been frosty between us of late, they had still called upon me to accompany them on their nocturnal missions of mischief. I was somewhat dis-chuffed by their decision to leave me behind. If there had been one thing that had kept me sane throughout my time in the school it had been the knowledge that in small ways I had been getting my own back on the powers that be with my little pranks. Over the years I had put boot polish on telephone ear pieces, stolen booze and pissed in teapots to name but a few of the crimes I had committed. If I wasn't going to be able to continue with my nocturnal crimes I thought I might go mad. They were all I had. I could not let that happen.

I climbed out of bed and silently crept after them keeping a safe distance. I watched as they snuck into the ablution block. I ran and hid around the side of the building in case there were any teachers o the prowl. I stood on my tiptoes and peeked through the window. In the gloom I could just make out the shape of them near the showers so I crept around to another window where I had a better vantage point. What I saw shocked me. They were both naked. Luke was lying on top of Joe. I knew this sort of thing was rife in school but I never suspected these two. It wasn't long ago that they were beating the hell out of Rubbish to get him to confess to being 'bent'. Even at that age I was aware that these couplings meant nothing. There were no girls in our lives and teenage boys were full of hormones and curiosity. Any hole was a goal as far as most of them were concerned. Still, I thought it best to hold out for a real girl. I had my doubts that it would ever happen, but I could dream.

As I had already stuffed my bed and was outside I thought I'd have a go at something on my own to see how it felt. I headed down to the staff dining room, flipped the window latch with my pen-knife and helped myself to some of the deputy-head's Sugar Puffs. After a lot of fumbling about I eventually got to grips with the percolator and made myself a cup of proper coffee. I took my drink, along with one of the woodwork teacher's cigarettes that were on the table, and went and sat down on the doorstep facing the hills. It was cold and the drizzling rain swept across the distant hills in sheets. As I wrapped my dressing gown tightly around me I felt alive and optimistic. I had rarely been able to find time to be on my own somewhere that I could relax and let my guard down. I didn't need Joe and Luke.

I dutifully washed my cup and made sure there was no evidence of my being there. As I was about to leave I shook a few drops of piss into the headmaster's cup and spread it around with my finger so that it would be obvious. I sniffed the cup. The smell of urine was barely discernable. I knew I'd get away with that one.

When I got back to the dormitory Joe and Luke were already back in their beds asleep. I climbed into bed feeling contented and confident that I would survive.

My mum, who was half Polish, half Irish, once told me the story of Genghis Khan. As a result of his army's invasion of Poland many of the women in the country fell pregnant. Subsequently, a large proportion of Poles were directly descended from the Mongols who had taken a shine to the womenfolk. I apparently had the high cheekbones and small eyes that were prevalent in the invaders' features. The belief that I was a direct descendant of such a mighty leader helped me get though the toughest of times. I was a warrior. There was nothing that they could do to me that would break me. Let them try.

Chapter 35

It was the Friday afternoon maths test. For fourth and fifth years this was always taken by the headmaster, who I personally saw as the most dangerous of all the teachers. Most of them filled me with a sense of dread when I was in their presence but the head particularly made my insides turn to ice. I felt there was always a hint of malicious glee whenever he deemed it necessary to chastise a child.

As an incentive to acquiring good scores in the maths test, the headmaster would award those with less than 50% three of the cane on each hand. His weapon of choice was usually the strap, but for some reason he liked to use the cane in maths. I detested the subject, probably in no small part due to who took the class, and I rarely got above half marks.

As soon as he started the clock I panicked as was usually the case and my mind went blank. I had spent all of the previous night memorising the formula for a quadratic equation, x = minus b plus or minus the square root of b squared all over 4ac. We had been studying it all week so the test was bound to primarily consist of questions on this subject. I looked at the question paper. Logarithms. I had forgotten my log book. Great. I was having trouble with my fountain pen as well. In no classes were we permitted ballpoint pens. My fountain pen was not one of the best. It had a plastic ink cartridge which I would struggle to get in properly and it would habitually leak onto the page, as it proceeded to so now.

"Put down your pens and pass your answer papers to the front," said the head. I couldn't believe that half an hour had passed so quickly. I surveyed my work and noticed that not only had I inevitably got most of my answers wrong, but it didn't look like I had even answered half of the questions. I had been on the receiving end of this man's cane and strap more times than I cared to remember, but I still felt that familiar sense of dread as my shaking hand passed my paper to the boy in front.

"Come back here after P.E. for your results. Off you go," said the head. With a heavy heart I made my way over to the gym hall.

As I was getting changed it became apparent that someone had nicked my shorts. That's all I need, I thought. I quickly scanned the room to see if there was anybody who hadn't turned up yet. I noticed that Slash was absent and instantly had a dilemma on my hands. Sod it! I thought, grabbed his shorts off the shelf without anybody noticing and got changed. I tried to convince myself that I was at no risk of being infected by his condition, but truth be told I didn't perform as well in P.E. as I should have. That said, it wasn't Slash's finest hour, having to do hand-springs over the vault in his underpants. It gave me some solace.

The P.E teacher decided, as usual, to prove his toughness and manliness by demonstrating his prowess in the gymnasium. He ran up to the springboard with the grace of a panther, executed a magnificent handspring, miscalculated the landing and ended up flat on his face. I couldn't help but laugh. He looked up, his face scarlet.

"Think that's bloody funny, do you, you little shit?" he shouted as he marched up to me. He delivered an almighty slap against the side of my face. It didn't hurt much but sounded like a gunshot as it sent me sprawling across the floor. "Come to the English classroom for detention after school," he said. "Let's see how funny you find that." There was a loud ringing in my left ear that reminded me of somebody rubbing their finger around the rim of a glass.

On my way to detention I dropped by the Maths class to pick up the result of my Maths test. Having turned up for the test without my log book my result was as I had predicted, nil. I asked the headmaster if I could have both lashes of the cane on my left hand as I needed my right hand to do lines with. He kindly acquiesced with my request. When I turned up for my detention an hour later my ear was still ringing and I was beginning to wonder if it would be permanent. Two other boys were there, Snotson from the fifth form and some first year I didn't recognise. I realised that nobody actually knew anybody from the years below (unless they publicly did something spectacularly stupid) but we all knew the kids who were older than us. It was due to this realisation that I deemed it totally unnecessary to speak to either of them. I couldn't be bothered with the first year and by the same token I knew the fifth year would only treat me with the same disdain. I took my seat. The P.E teacher walked in. I noticed that he never changed out of the orange tracksuit he was wearing and thought how he must stink.

"You all know why you're here," he began with the usual boring spiel. "But I'm going to give you the opportunity to come up with your own line which must be repeated five hundred times before you leave. It'll give you the chance to look inside yourselves to see what's wrong with your attitudes. Hopefully it might make you into better people."

That's rather deep for a fucking orang-utan, I thought. I began by writing that I must not laugh at people who have no sense of humour, but self-preservation prevailed and came up with the line that I must not anger teachers, which I thought was a stroke of genius as it told the bastard what he wanted to hear yet it was only five words long. Everyone's a winner, I though and merrily ploughed into the task. I finished well before the other boys and put up my hand to leave.

"What?" he demanded.

"I've finished sir, can I go now?"

"You can't have bloody finished. Bring it here." I took the lines up to his desk. He does smell, I thought as I got close to him.

"Are you taking the piss?" he asked.

"No sir," I said.

He squinted as he looked up to me.

"Quite arrogant really, aren't you?" he said.

"Thank you sir," I replied. I wasn't being facetious, I'd heard my mum telling my dad that he was arrogant and he usually smiled at her accusation. I therefore genuinely thought that it was a good thing.

"That isn't a compliment," he said. "Tell me, what do the other boys call you?"

"Er, Stonekicker sir."

"Why's that then?" he seemed genuinely interested.

"I think it's because I choose to spend time on my own a lot," I replied.

"Ah, I think I get it," he said. "Not because you're a pathetic, spineless fool who can't get anybody to like him?" he suggested.

That's a bit low, even for a teacher, I thought.

"Not at all, sir."

"Get back to the dormitory," he said. "I can't bear to look at you anymore."

As I walked out of the classroom I noticed both of the other boys watching me. I stuck my fingers up at them both and instantly regretted it as I now knew I had made another bloody enemy in Snotson. Ah well, I thought, never mind. Still, on the plus side, I hadn't had to do P.E. in my pants. Every cloud…

I had got back to the dormitory and just had time to get changed when it was teatime. I was upset at having missed the chance to copy some song lyrics out of Luke's music magazine, which had been my original plan after finishing school. Some other bugger had just borrowed it from him and I seemed destined to be forever unable to sing along with the song when it came on the radio. I was gutted. There would be no time to get it later as we had prep after tea then bed. The thought of prep made me realise that I hadn't managed to get the Maths homework answers from Skid. I desperately needed them or I would get into even more trouble. God forbid I try to figure the answers out for myself during the impending two hours supervised prep. Way too boring. Skid had a natural flair for Maths and it was only fair that he share his talent. I collared him nursing his left hand on the way back from tea.

"What's the matter?" I asked.

"I put my elbow on the table and got salt-potted for it," he replied.

"Twat," I said. "Hey, don't suppose I could borrow your Maths homework could I? I'll give it you back after prep."

"Can't, I've lent it to Jelly Belly and Clock's after him."

"Bollocks," I replied and walked off in search of one of the other boffins who were, unfortunately, in very short supply and high in demand. I got back to the dormitory and spotted Clock straining to tip somebody's bed over.

"Have you got Skid's Maths homework on you?" I

asked.

"No, I've given it to Turd-breath, you'll have to ask him," he said, wiping sweat from his overly large forehead.

"Can't I just borrow yours if you're done with it?"

"Fuck off! Can't you see I'm busy?"

"Keep your hair on," I said.

"Oh yeah, Stonekicker," called Clock. "I think you've learnt your lesson now, so we'll call it quits. But think twice in future about pissing me off, ok?

"Yeah, cheers," I replied. Rot in hell.

I wandered off in search of Turd-breath and eventually found him in the ablution block brushing his teeth (again).

"Can I borrow Skid's Maths homework off you," I asked.

"What's it worth?"

"I've got some extra strong mints in my locker."

"Fuck off!" I'd been getting a lot of that lately. I returned to the dormitory and found Turd-breath's bedside locker. I rummaged through it until I found his school books. I took Skid's Maths book and wrote 'See me after class' in red ink inside Turd-breath's book. I went to my bed and started copying the homework. Turd-breath walked into the dorm and approached me.

"Where did you get that from? Have you been in my locker, you fucking Billy-no-mates bender?"

I stood up to face him. He was a couple of inches shorter than me but very stocky. I didn't rate my chances.

"I'm not a bender, and besides, I caught Slash nicking it from your cupboard and I rescued it for you, so I think you owe me an apology," I said.

"Fucking liar," he said and kicked me in the balls. As I doubled over in pain I tried to contain an imminent outburst but failed.

"Not only does your breath stink of shit, but you've got a mouth like a toilet," I blurted. He kicked me in the ribs. I winced as I felt my unhealed rib give again. "And you kick like a girl," I added before falling on my bed. He then began raining punches on me in fury.

"Oy, leave him alone, he's alright." I looked up to see my saviour. It was the kid I'd stolen the soldiers from.

"Do you fucking want some, you spastic?" Turd-breath turned to face the boy.

"I'm not a spastic!" Windowlicker shouted as he swung his satchel at Turd-breath. Being full of books as well as his box of toy soldiers the bag was of a formidable weight. It knocked Turd-breath off his feet and face first into the wall where he slid down into a bloody-faced heap on the floor.

"I think you've killed him," somebody remarked.

I walked up to him and looked down. He wasn't moving. I kicked him in the head. He groaned.

"Nah, he's alright," I said and nodded a secret acknowledgement of gratitude to Windowlicker.

"You've got a bit of a thing for spazzes, haven't you?" said Jelly-belly who was watching from his bed while smearing bogies on his headboard.

"Don't you fucking start, you fat bastard," I replied.

"Or what?" he said, standing up. Windowlicker stepped forward and Jelly-belly sat back down again. My new predicament had left me in quite a state of confusion.

Chapter 36

The next day we had Maths. Luckily I had got around to copying it all in time for the lesson. We all walked in and placed our exercise books on the headmaster's desk before taking our seats.

"Open your books to page eighty-four and complete questions j to q. I don't need to tell you to do it in silence, do I?"

"No sir," we all chanted dutifully. I sat down and got out my books. I looked up at the headmaster who was busy marking our homework and flicked some chewed-up paper at the boy in front from my ruler. When he turned around I looked behind me to give him the impression that somebody else had done it. As I turned back to the front there was a sharp pain in my forehead as the wooden board rubber hit me right between the eyes.

"Get on with your work," the headmaster said casually as he came and retrieved his weapon.

At the end of the class he called out about ten names telling them to stay behind. Mine was among them, as was Skid's to my surprise. He called Skid to the front first.

"I must say, looking at your homework, that I'm bewildered. For somebody who consistently scores over ninety per-cent it amazes me that this time you've only managed to score twenty-seven per-cent. What amazes me even more is the fact that all of the boys behind you, without exception, have also scored twenty-seven per-cent on this occasion," he said.

"Sorry sir. I must have been having a bad day," said Skid. He then glanced at the rest of us with what I was sure was a slight grin on his face. The little bastard, I thought. He's done this on purpose to stop us all pestering him for his homework.

"Well, be that as it may, you've scored less than half marks and you know what that means."

"Yes sir," he replied and stuck out his hand. He got one lash of the cane on each hand. He didn't flinch. As I stood in line for my punishment I kind of admired him for the stance he had taken. We all got an extra lash for copying.

On the way back to the dorm one boy pointed out an observation he had made.

"Was I the only one who noticed he had a hard-on when he was caning us?"

"Yeah, I noticed that," said another.

I knew the headmaster liked punishing us but I didn't believe anybody could take that much pleasure in their work.

Chapter 37

None of us are noble beings. Many of us like to believe that we are good people, but there is not one of us alive who hasn't in some way scarred somebody else out of sheer malice. We choose to condemn the actions of others while forgetting the crimes we have committed over the years. I won't. For me, it was perpetrating these sins that helped me to become a more understanding empathetic person. Many people do not behave in such ways as children and tend to make these mistakes as adults. This is worse. As a child our desires are simple and the crimes we commit to achieve our aims are, while not entirely harmless, ultimately simple too. As an adult we are so much more capable of real damage. The malicious acts we perform can lead to heartache, death and a loss of everything that people hold dear. I like to think that I committed these crimes early in life and learnt from my mistakes. We can all redeem ourselves if we so choose. But while I wholeheartedly believe that corporal punishment did not, in the long run, do me any great harm, I do know for a fact that physical abuse did me no good at all. I only grew out of this type of bad behaviour by the positive influences in my life, those people who could see the smallest amount of goodness in me and encouraged it to grow by treating me with decency. These were the role models I had. Sometimes the motivation for their positive influence did not come from the purest of sources. Nevertheless it was these acts of kindness that helped me to grow. I like to think that the paths I have chosen to take in life, the acts of good I have done, have more than made up for the atrocious behaviour I displayed as a child. But even if that is the case, I apologise. And if I have offended any of the teachers at the school by revealing their despicable nature, well, they're probably all dead by now. And as far as speaking ill of the dead is concerned, well, they asked for it.

Chapter 38

Rubbish defied the laws of the nickname. Every time somebody called him by his nickname he fought against it, telling them to call him by his real name, Sean. This only served to make them to call him Rubbish all the more and often led to a beating. But he never gave up. He was a strange one but I felt a certain kinship with him due to his rebellious streak.

I was on my own one day, scraping mud from my football boots in the outside sink by the gym. It was freezing and my fingers were numbing as I tried to dig between the studs. There was a sudden pain at the back of my legs. My knees buckled and I fell to the floor. My numbed hands hitting the floor sent a wave of sharp pain through my arms. I got to my knees and looked up to see Rubbish standing over me with a yard brush in his hands.

"Hello Marcus," he said, smiling.

"Rubbish. What are you playing at? That fucking hurt."

"It's Sean," he replied simply.

"Sean. What are you doing?"

"Teaching you a lesson. You're pathetic."

"Look," I said. I think it's Luke and Joe you need to talk to."

"I don't think so. At least they had the courage of their convictions to do what they did. You knew it was wrong and you still did it. You haven't got the backbone to be your own man." He swung the broom and hit me across the back. I fell on my face and scraped my chin on the tarmac.

"I'm sorry," I said. The pain in my back was excruciating.

"Are you bent?" he asked.

"Yeah, of course I am. Whatever you say."

"Say it." He hit me on the head.

"Fucksake, that hurt. Alright, alright, I'm bent ok?"

He looked up at the sky for a second as if pondering something. I had the opportunity to sweep his feet out from under him but didn't take it. I figured he was justified. I didn't like hearing it, but I thought he had a point. I had been weak.

"That's more like it." He leaned down and picked up one of my football boots. "There's still mud on this," he said and threw it onto the gym roof. He laughed to himself and walked back towards the dormitory. I dragged myself to my feet and tried to figure out how I was going to retrieve my boot. I spotted Windowlicker walking by the dining hall and beckoned him over. He was only too happy to offer me a bunk-up so that I could reach the edge of the roof. I swung my legs up and I was there. I had just spotted my football boot on the far side of the flat roof when I heard someone shout.

"Get down off that roof, right now!" It was the Geography teacher. He was about forty feet away and approaching fast. He was far enough away not to be able to identify me. I dropped to my belly and listened as he came running towards the gym.

"Who's that up there?" he demanded.

"Don't know sir," replied Windowlicker. Nice one Windowlicker, I thought.

"What do you mean, you don't bloody know?" the teacher shouted. "I just saw you lift him up to get on there."

"I don't know his name sir," Windowlicker insisted.

"Get out of my sight," said the teacher. I heard Windowlicker's footsteps as he walked away. "There are going to be serious consequences if you don't get down off that roof, right now," he yelled at me. No chance, I thought.

I wished he would hurry up and go, my bare feet were freezing. He wouldn't give up though. He just shouted threat after threat. A crowd was starting to gather and I was beginning to get a bit worried.

"What's going on here?" It was the headmaster. Christ, I thought, this is going from bad to worse.

"There's a boy on the roof, Headmaster," replied the teacher.

"Get off that roof this instant," shouted the headmaster. "Who is the boy?" he asked the Geography teacher.

"I didn't get to see his face, Headmaster."

Ha! I was right. He didn't know who it was. I had a brainwave. I couldn't believe I hadn't though of it earlier. I crept across the roof and grabbed my football boot. I then crept to the far side of the roof and peeked over the edge. There was nobody there! I gripped the edge, hung down and dropped to the ground. My feet hurt as I landed but I was alright. I walked around to join the crowd on the other side of the building, feigning curiosity. I was just in time. I could see the P.E. teacher speaking to the headmaster. He nodded at something he said then got a bunk-up from the geography teacher. I surreptitiously bent down and retrieved the boot I had left behind.

"Whoever it was has gone, Headmaster," he called down.

"Very well," the headmaster sighed. "Everybody return to your dorms, there's nothing to see here." The crowd groaned and I headed back to the dorm with a skip in my step. I had forgotten all about my little altercation with Rubbish, or Sean, as I began to call him from that day on.

Chapter 39

One Saturday afternoon in the village, Joe and Luke found me and came over to join me on a wall eating chips and watching the local girls go by. I could have done without the company, I'd gone off the pair of them, and besides, they'd only cramp my style with the girls. There were three of them sitting on a bench on the other side of the road. None of us had the courage to approach them so we just sat on the wall trying to look cool. I was fifteen years old and had still never kissed a girl.

When I was about eight there was a girl in one of the flats downstairs who invited me in one day. She took me into her room and told me to take my socks off. She then took off her socks. Although it never progressed to anything more sensuous, there was definitely an electric charge which we both felt. It was the most erotic experience I had had to that day.

Needless to say, I didn't have a clue about how to impress a girl, but I thought I'd give it a go. There were two men talking about ten feet away from us. One of them had a collie dog. I beckoned it to come to me by waving a chip at it. As it approached I threw the chip into the middle of the road. The dog followed. A driver slammed his brakes on to avoid hitting it. The owner witnessed the whole thing. He came up to me screaming, asking what kind of monster I was before clouting me really hard across the side of my head. The girls weren't impressed. They just sneered at me in disgust and walked away.

"Well done," said Joe.

On the way back to school we stopped off at the sporting goods shop. We looked around for five minutes trying to determine what might come in handy. The darts that the school provided in the games room were the cheapest money could buy with blunt tips and plastic flights. I spotted some really fancy expensive ones in the shop. I gave Joe the nod and he went up to the shopkeeper and asked him some technical questions about snooker cues while I grabbed about half a dozen sets of darts. Having achieved our objective without being caught we made our way out of the shop, climbed over the fence down the road and into the field that would lead us back to school.

We passed some first years who were on their way down to the village. They all dutifully nodded to us as they passed. I turned around and threw a dart into the backside of one of the boys. He howled more in surprise than pain at what I had done. I was amazed at his bravery as he removed the dart instinctively and threw it full force towards my face. I put up my hand and watched in what felt like slow motion as the point of the dart went right through my hand. The group of boys saw what he had done and all ran down the hill as fast as their legs could carry them.

I regarded the dart curiously. It barely hurt and there was no blood.

"Well, you can't say you didn't ask for that," said Joe.

"No," I said. "Fair play to the little bastard." I then promptly sat down hard on the grass as my legs gave way. "Are you alright if we just sit here for a while?" I asked.

My hand was starting to throb. I winced as I grabbed hold of the dart's shaft and pulled out the dart. I gripped my hand tight in a fist and looked at it. There was blood trickling slowly out of the back of it.

"That doesn't seem too bad," I said and opened my palm. A thin jet of blood squirted about two feet into the air. I clenched my fist again. The bleeding stopped.

"You might want to get that looked at," said Joe.

When we arrived back at the school Joe led me in a daze to the Sick Bay. The matron came to greet us.

"What have you done?" she asked looking down at my blood-soaked hand.

"Tripped and fell on a nail down the village, Miss," I replied.

"Let me have a look then." She grabbed my hand and prized my fingers open. The bleeding had slowed and my palm looked a little bit like a burst sausage, the flesh inside protruding from the wound. She soon ascertained that nothing inside had been damaged.

"You've had you're tetanus booster, haven't you?" she asked. She was already preparing a needle.

"I think so." We'd queued up and been jabbed so many times without even being told what the injections were for, that I had no idea what I was protected against. She jabbed me again 'to be on the safe side.' She then cleaned my wound and prepared another needle.

"What's that for?"

"It's an anaesthetic. I'm going to need to put a stitch in that. You'd better sit down for this one." I sat, feeling a little bit anxious. She made me put out my hand then thrust a needle into the wound and injected the anaesthetic. I passed out.

I was still sitting in the chair when I regained consciousness. Joe was in tears of laughter.

"How long was I out for?"

"Only a few seconds," replied the Matron. She put some steri-strips on the back of my hand and stuck a needle and thread into the palm of my hand and stitched the hole closed. This didn't hurt at all. It fascinated me. When she finished we were sent back to the dormitory.

"Are you going to get the kid that did that to you?" asked Joe. "I'd kick his head in for that."

"No. I'll tell him he's dead meat if he brags about it, but at the end of the day I did ask for it."

Suffering the pain of an object being forced through my hand made me feel a little bit like Jesus. I thought that was probably why I was in such a forgiving mood. I walked the rest of the way back admiring my war wound and priding myself on my niceness.

Joe and Luke were starting to grow on me again. For the time being.

Chapter 40

It was Saturday morning. Games. In my previous life the word 'games' was always associated with fun. Now it sent shivers down my spine. If the Saturday games had been athletics or swimming I would have loved it. I was good at those. But it always had to be team sports, didn't it? Football, Rugby, Cricket. I hated those. I wasn't a 'team' kind of kid. The weather had improved and it ended up being cricket. Although I wasn't averse to a bit of pain the prospect of a hard leather cricket ball hitting me in the mouth at a hundred miles an hour made me shudder. I'd seen it happen to a boy before. The over-zealous P.E. teacher batted the ball straight into his face from a distance of about ten yards. The boy lost most of his teeth and suffered a broken nose. He ended up being nicknamed Quasi. Cricket also bored me senseless. How on earth did trying to knock somebody's head off with a cricket ball make it the 'sport for gentlemen'? Maybe it was the white trousers and V-neck jumper that made it seem less savage. To me it was like motor racing – not worth watching unless there's a horrific accident. I didn't have a clue about scoring or the terminology. It was rubbish.

I was standing at the bottom of the field 'fielding', praying that the ball wouldn't head my way. It did. The batsman hit it high into the air and it was obviously going to come down where I was standing. Catching it would mean winning the match. Everybody was screaming at me in excitement. Bastards. My heart was pounding. I looked up to track the ball's trajectory but the sun blinded me. I had horrible flashbacks to the boy who'd been disfigured by the ball. I caught sight of it just in time and managed to dodge out of the way before it hit me. It landed on the grass with a dull thud and the opposing team roared. My side however, weren't quite as happy with my performance.

"Coward!"

"Puff!"

"Why didn't you catch it, you spaz?" The angry mob was baying for my blood. At least my face was intact. Still, I was a bit concerned that I might be in for a tough time for the foreseeable future.

We were herded into the shower by the headmaster, who had taken us for cricket on this occasion. Most of us covered our bits with our soapboxes as we knew what he was like. I walked out of the shower noticing that the head was absent. I spotted Huey in front of me and wondered if having a wet back would make the red, hand-shaped mark left by a sharp back-slap all the more vivid. I decided to find out. Before he could spot me I crept up and gave him the most almighty smack on his back. Lo and behold, the imprint that my hand left on his back was so magnificent you could almost see the swirls of my fingerprints. He howled, hopping about on one foot as if that was where the pain was coming from. Everybody found this hilarious and somebody flicked his backside with a wet towel for good measure. This served to increase the pitch of his scream. I seemed to have got the crowd back on-side after my dreadful performance on the cricket pitch, field, whatever you call it. Genius. The headmaster walked into the room and spotted the hand print on his back.

"Who did that to you," he asked the boy. He pointed at me. The head came up to me and gave me four sharp taps on the back of my head. "Don't" slap "do" slap "it" slap "again" slap.

"Sorry sir," I said. Fuck off and die.

I walked into the changing rooms and began to towel

myself dry. The headmaster had moved on. I put the towel around my waist and walked up to Huey offering my hand.

"Sorry mate." He looked up at me with tears still in his eyes. He tentatively took my hand. I grabbed and twisted, bending his arm backwards with enough pressure to lift him off the ground. I dropped him and he screamed. The headmaster walked back in and glared at him. Oh shit, I thought.

"Who the bloody hell was it this time laddie?" he asked him.

"Him again, sir," he snivelled. You bastard, I thought. The headmaster practically ran at me and punched me in the face. I fell to the floor.

"Get up!" he shouted then kicked me in the side. "Think you're bloody tough, do you. Come on, get up you bloody coward." I staggered to my feet. Get over to my office!" He shoved me out of the door and my towel caught on the handle. I was outside the building naked. There were about a hundred yards between where I was and his office. He punched and kicked me all the way there. We reached his office and he shoved me inside. I was crying; more from the humiliation than anything else.

"I'm sorry, sir," I whimpered.

"Not so bloody tough now are you?" he said. "Look at yourself. You make me sick, picking on those smaller than yourself. I've a good mind to expel you here and now. Would you like that?"

Yes I bloody well would, I thought.

"No sir," I replied.

"Put your hand out." He took his strap out of a drawer.

He was panting and sweating as he administered the first lash. There was an evil expression of glee on his face.

He took his time between each lash to ensure that the pain had time to register. I'd stopped crying by this time. If there was one thing I was intent on doing it was to make sure that he could see his brutality was ineffective. He finished and leant forward and put his hands on the desk. The whole ordeal had obviously taken its toll on him. Go on, I thought, have a heart attack.

"Get out," he gasped. I walked back to the changing room with one hand over my backside and one covering my front in a futile attempt to maintain some decency. As I walked in the room everybody looked at me. Nobody laughed. Even the biggest arseholes seemed too shocked to say anything.

"It's a bit fresh out there," I said, trying to break the ice. Luke gave me a forced smile. I noticed Huey was still sniffing in the corner of the room.

"Oh, get a fucking grip," I said to him.

It was a real struggle getting changed. The headmaster's strap was only about a foot long and very thick. When it hit me the pain was doubled. The fronts of my hands were stinging to high heaven but the backs of my hands were swollen from where the tip of the strap had flicked around and caught them. I just about managed to get my clothes on but Luke had to help me with my tie as my hands were still shaking violently. On the bright side, everybody seemed to have totally forgotten about my shameful performance in the cricket match. Swings and roundabouts.

I spent the rest of the day pondering over whether or not I was being victimised. It was always me that suffered the most at the hands of the teachers. Apart from the time I saw the woodwork teacher rip an 'unauthorised' earring straight through the ear lobe of one unfortunate boy; I didn't think I had seen anybody get treated as badly as me. It really wasn't very fair. After all, I'd only been having a laugh.

Chapter 41

As we approached the Easter holidays in our last year in the school we were visited by the police. There was a real buzz in the school as all the boys speculated as to what the visit might mean. The reason soon became apparent. I was sitting in the maths block trying to muster enthusiasm with a quadratic equation when I glanced out of the window. Three uniformed policemen were escorting Mr McEwan to a waiting police car. He wore a lost expression on his face as one of the officers gently held his head and eased him into the back of the car.

They called for us all one by one. I was one of the first. They sat me down in the headmaster's office with the head standing behind his desk listening. There were two middle aged policemen who both smiled and told me not to worry.

"Before we start we just want to let you know that you're not in trouble for anything." Even after what I had just witnessed I breathed a sigh of relief. I had a huge stash of butter from the staff room hidden in my tuck box and I was still convinced that they had found it and were going to throw the book at me.

"Ok," I said.

"Now, could you tell us how you get on with Mr McEwan?" one of them asked.

What the bloody hell are they going on about? Why had they arrested him? "Alright," I said.

"Has he ever been alone with you?"

"I dunno Officer," I replied. Do I call him Officer or Constable? I was nervous and thought I might giggle if I called him Constable as it sounded a bit like Cunt. I tried to get back on track with the subject in hand. I wasn't going to drop Mr McEwan in the shit for whatever they thought he'd done.

"Has he ever touched you?"

"He slippered me once in the first year,"

"No. We mean in a way that you found uncomfortable," said the policeman.

I hadn't considered the slippering to be particularly comfortable but I had an idea that I knew where this was heading.

"Definitely not," I replied. It's the bastard standing behind you that you want to look at, I wanted to say. He's a fucking sadist who likes to stare at you when you're in the shower. If anyone's a deviant it's him. But I was too scared to say it.

It seemed that Mr McEwan was being investigated for molesting some of the schoolboys. I didn't believe it. It had to be some malicious little bastards making false allegations. He was ok. Even if it was true, which I strongly doubted, however depraved his motivation he had never touched me and had been one of the most positive influences in my life, someone who made me feel worthy and good and special. This experience was horrible. There were so many of the other teachers who were infinitely worse than him in my opinion.

The interview ended and I returned to the classroom feeling hollow. The other boys swarmed around me to find out what had happened but I couldn't bring myself to speak about it. For the next two days all of the boys in the school were interviewed. By the end of the week we were told that Mr McEwan had gone for good, as had three of the boys. Rumour had it that he had been sent to prison. Many of the boys rejoiced at the fact that we had finally got back at one of the teachers. Accusations flew against many of the other staff in the school but the police were never summoned again. The replacement for Mr McEwan seemed to be just like the rest of the teachers. The stories and essays I wrote in class were not met with the warmth and enthusiasm of his predecessor. Any form of creativity displayed by any of the boys was stifled by derisory comments. The teacher would read out our work in class adding a sarcastic tone to his recitals which had the other boys laughing in scorn. 'Unrealistic, immature and far-fetched' were just some of the heavy words that were so casually thrown at my work. I gave up trying in the end. It came to my attention that he wasn't even reading the most of the essays I submitted. I tested this by inserting inappropriate words or sentences in the middle of my work: 'In my opinion the protagonist of this novel continued to maintain his dignity even as he approached the gallows. The English teacher is a twat. He would look down at the crowd of peasants baying for his blood and still possess an air of authority that would command their rapt attention'. I got a C minus for that one. Never once were my derisory comments noticed which proved one of two things: either the teacher was incredibly tolerant and agreed with my comments or he never even bothered reading the work I handed in. I suspected the latter.

    I did have an unusual reaction to the dismissal of Mr McEwan. My hatred towards the bullies and the teachers intensified. It occurred to me that it was their disgusting behaviour and wild accusations that were responsible for the destruction of another person's life. The violent behaviour displayed by the boys was just the knock-on effect of the bullish conduct exhibited by the teachers. I empathised with the poor kids who were always the victims, slightly. If there was one thing that Mr McEwan taught me, it was that I didn't need the approval of my peers to feel special. I no longer cared about currying favour with the other boys. I decided to spend my last few months in the school getting my own back on them all. I thought a lot about how disgusted my mother and Mr McEwan would have been at some of my earlier behaviour. I thought about my uncle and grandparents and how I had alienated them in favour of the approval of peers who I didn't give a shit about. I couldn't change the past but I wanted to do something. I seemed to have lost all of my humanity and had become some kind of self-centred feral animal. I knew that I had seen that behaviour as a survival tool but the end was now in sight and I wasn't prepared to compromise my integrity any more. I hoped that this epiphany wouldn't be as fleeting as its failed predecessors. It kind of was. The fury was replaced with a weary resignation. But I did change. I wasn't going to fight anymore. I really couldn't be arsed.

Chapter 42

I was sitting in Technical Drawing one day trying to figure out how to draw a zeppelin with compasses when there was a knock on the classroom door. A first year came in and told the teacher that the headmaster wanted to see me. Oh God, I thought, what has the bastard caught me doing now? I walked down to his office trying to will my legs to stop shaking.

As I approached the office door I became convinced that I hadn't left any of my 'acquisitions' anywhere they could incriminate me and therefore somebody must have reported me for something. In school the 'Grasses' were deemed by the pupils to be on a moral par with the child molesting teachers. I would find the bugger responsible. I walked into the office and realised that the last time I had come in here I had been naked. Less said about that the better, I thought.

"Sit down laddie," said the head. I was gobsmacked. He had *never* offered me a chair before. Shit, he's going to suspend me, I thought. Ah well, I suppose I've had it coming. Although the prospect of being at home and having no school appealed to me tremendously, I couldn't bear the thought of upsetting my mother. I sat resignedly.

"What have I done, sir?" I asked.

"Your grandmother's dead."

"Oh." Which one? I thought.

"Now, as your G.C.E's are approaching I'm going to let you go home the day before the funeral, which I believe is next Tuesday, but you must be back the following day so as not to miss too much school."

"Ok." I was actually taking more C.S.E's than G.C.E's, but I thought it'd be best not to quibble.

"Now off you go, back to class."

I walked out of his office in a state of shock. I was relieved that I had come out of the visit unscathed but I couldn't fathom what had really happened.

The following Monday I came out of the last class to be greeted in the car park by my dad. It had turned out to be his mother that had died. He didn't bring my uncle with him so I felt safe taking him to the dormitory to collect my stuff.

"Been in much trouble lately?" he asked. He was the only one I could confide in when it came to confessing my misdemeanours and subsequent punishments. Although he used to beat the living shit out of me as a child for the most ridiculous of reasons, i.e. I once changed the channel on the TV and he attacked me in a frenzy with his belt, he was actually quite proud of my delinquent behaviour at school. He would often regale me with tales of his own misspent youth.

"A bit," I replied.

"Just make sure the bastards don't catch you, and remember what I told you about the other kids; if any of them hit you, then hit them back twice as hard."

"Gotcha."

He put my case in the boot of his American sports car and roared out of the school at about a hundred miles an hour. I watched the other kids and teachers stare in awe and dismay respectively and felt as happy as a pig in shit as we flew out of the gates.

The funeral was a predictably sombre affair. I quite enjoyed the experience of being away from school, dressing smartly and drinking beer at the wake. Relatives who I had not seen in years kept coming up to me commenting on how much I had grown and how much I looked like my dad. That comment has always slightly grated on me for some reason. My dad would tell them all how well I was doing at boarding school, but how it was against his wishes that I went there in the first place and how he had always wanted me to live with him.

Lying bugger, I thought. If he had been a bit more forthcoming with the maintenance my mother may have had other options. I guess neither of them was fully equipped with the necessary tools required to be successful parents at that age.

My granddad just seemed to wander around aimlessly, shaking hands and nodding at all the right moments. When people left his company it was always with a worried frown on their face. I tried to engage him in conversation at one point but it felt too awkward and difficult so I left him there and returned to my dad who wasn't in a much better mood. It became so that it was almost a relief to return to school the next day.

Two weeks later I was summoned to the headmaster's office again. In his usual callous fashion he informed me that my granddad had followed my grandma to the grave. Being only days away from my exams he was rather irritated by the fact that I had to go to another funeral.

This time it hit both me and my father really hard. Even though we were both closer to my grandma than my granddad I guess we both realised the hole that was in our lives now that both of them had gone. I remembered that my last letter to my grandparents before they died was just a request for money, no concern for their well-being whatsoever.

At the funeral Philip was going around saying that his mum and dad were in heaven and he was the man of the house now. He didn't seem to realise that he wouldn't be able to look after himself there and it would be necessary for him to move to a care home. Distant relatives were offering him their condolences and empty promises to keep in touch. My dad promised him that he would always be there for him. I knew that these reassurances were equally without substance. I also knew that it was the end of my relationship with him and that this would be through my own despicable neglect.

I was whizzed back to school the next day. I was told what I had missed and advised to knuckle down and start revising for the impending examinations. I really couldn't be arsed. I was despondent and resented the fact that I was stuck in that hellhole when I could have spent time with my grandparents before they died. As the headmaster spoke to us in assembly the next day about how these results would affect the rest of our lives and we must not let ourselves be distracted, I just wanted to stab the bastard in the face. I wanted to get the exams over and done with so I could get out of the fucking place forever.

That night I went to bed wearing a pair of pyjamas that my dad had given me on the day I came back. They had been my granddad's. I didn't know if they were the ones he had died in but that didn't bother me. It was just nice to have something to remind me of him in that hellhole.

When the exams were over a fortnight later I grabbed my case and walked out of the gates without a backward glance. The results were not what my mum would have wanted for me. It would be cheap to blame my grandparents' deaths for my lack of success, I hadn't given much of a shit about my prospects before they died and couldn't imagine that I would have put in more effort if they hadn't.

It wasn't quite the exhilarating feeling that I expected as I walked towards the village to get the bus home. Not that I was going to miss the school, I just didn't know anything else and feared what the future might bring. I wished I had had the guts to confront some of the teachers and tell them what I thought of them before I left. I wished I could have had the know how to blow up the headmaster's house. Still, it was all over.

I boarded the bus for home and had an argument with the driver about the fact that I wasn't sixteen until August and should only pay half fare for the journey. I lost the argument and went and sat down at the back of the bus and lit a fag. I looked out of the window and up the road towards the school. On this balmy summer's day it looked resplendent in its position at the top of the hill. To somebody who didn't know any better it seemed just like the schools in the old books, where you could imagine midnight feasts and haughty but ultimately lovable teachers who would guide one's child down a path that would lead to great things. Shame that.

I tipped a stone out of my shoe and kicked it down the aisle.

REUNION

Twenty-five years after I had left the school Joe tracked me down and told me of a reunion. He wanted to know if I'd go along with him. It was to involve a day looking around the school and the surrounding area, followed by a get-together at the local pub. Many of the teachers would also be in attendance. For a small fee we were permitted to spend the night in one of the old dormitories. Curiosity got the better of me and I acquiesced.

Since leaving the school I had spent some time in the armed forces and had been a police officer for the last ten years. I had been happily married for many years and had two daughters, but when I drove through the school gates I felt like a child again.

My brother came along with me. Although he only spent a year in the place I could see that he too was feeling slightly anxious about the prospect of meeting old friends and foes. I didn't know what I felt more worried about, meeting people who had wronged me, be they teachers or pupils, or meeting the people I had wronged.

As everybody was left to their own devices until the reunion party that evening, my brother, Joe and I were able to roam the school grounds without being accosted. I heard the sound of a blown exhaust pipe as a car roared into the car park. It was a suped-up Herald. The driver had obviously tampered with the exhaust to get the hideous noise. I watched as he got out of the car.

"Isn't he that kid that was always beating people up?" asked my brother. The driver of the car approached me.

"Y'alright Stonekicker?" he said. "You haven't changed a bit."

"Hello Clock," I replied. He had changed. His

expanding gut spilt over his tight jeans. "You've been living the high life, by the look of it," I said sarcastically, nodding towards his midriff.

"Yeah," he said, patting his stomach affectionately. "All bought and paid for." He looked around dramatically. "I couldn't resist coming to this, he said. "We had some laughs, didn't we?"

Are you fucking serious? I thought.

"Yeah, happy days indeed," I lied. "Anyway, must dash. We've got a bit of exploring to do. See you later." I shook my head in despair and carried on checking the school out.

The school closed down the year I left due to lack of funding and was now home to a religious group who used the place as a kind of Christian out-of- bounds centre for kids. Most of the buildings were almost identical to how they were twenty-five years ago. I had expected to feel a warm nostalgia at seeing the place again after all of these years. I just felt a little bit sad and unsettled. I was also grateful for having escaped the school relatively unscathed. I was over half way through my life and had only spent a very small portion of it here, yet I felt the place still had a power over me now. Things I had done throughout the years, career choices I had made, I suddenly felt that they were all because of what had happened here, but not in a positive way. I was happy with my job and my family life, but I felt resentful that I had this happiness as a result of having to fight against the behavioural patterns and beliefs that the school tried to force on me for five years. That I had to scream at myself that I was worth a toss, that I could be loved, that I didn't have to respond to everything in my life with violence and animosity. I didn't have to have my guard up with everybody, always being suspicious of people. I didn't have to make other people suffer just to make my life seem that little bit better. I prayed that there were no vestiges of the school's influence still in me. But I wasn't so sure. To me, the school felt like a living, breathing entity, and the one thing in my life that tried to destroy who I was and turn me into a monster, which I feared it had succeeded in to some degree.

During the evening I pointed out to my brother the teachers who I felt had taken a sadistic pleasure in their duties. He walked up to the Science teacher. He was now a bent old man who now held a stick out of necessity. He was nearing the end of his life and I wondered how awkward he felt in the presence of the school boys who could now snap him in half like a dry twig.

"My brother tells me you used to beat him," said my brother with a wry grin on his face. The old man struggled to look up at me.

"Well, you must have needed it," he said. I just grinned.

"And he used to piss in your mug in the middle of the night!" he said to the old man.

"I didn't," I lied. "Take no notice of my brother, he's drunk." I grabbed my brother's arm and walked away fast, leaving the old man looking rather flustered.

It transpired that some of the teachers had died in the years since the school's closure. Even as a fully grown, hopefully mature man who had an ability to empathise with the worst kind of monster, I was glad. The headmaster could not make it to the reunion; I'd have been amazed if he did have the gall to show his face. I looked around. So many of the ex pupils seemed to be really enjoying themselves, deep in conversation with each other and the staff. It fascinated me how nostalgia could be felt for even the worst memories. Maybe I had it all wrong. Maybe I'd read evil intent in actions when it just wasn't there. Maybe the punishments inflicted were just a sign of the times. These people were actually innocent; just doing their jobs. I had spent all these years over-reacting. No, I couldn't swallow that. They knew what they were doing and they loved it.

There was a tap on my shoulder and I turned to see a familiar face.

"Still a Billy-no-mates, I see," said the short balding man in front of me.

"Hello," I said as the memories came back. "I see the nits won't be partying much in your hair these days."

"That was a bloody mistake, you know," he retorted. "I never bloody had nits in the first place. It was just one of the midges from outside. The old bag got it wrong and I ended up being Nit-boy for five years."

"Alright, keep your hair on," I said and turned to go and look at the old panoramic photos on the wall. I scanned the wall until I found one with my class. I noticed Mr McEwan sitting proudly next to the headmaster maintaining an austere demeanour in his mortar board and gown. I smiled at the memory of the kind way he used to treat me.

"He buggered my mate!" said the man standing next to me. I thought he was joking until I noticed his eyes were welling up.

"He was alright with me," I stated.

"What the fuck do you know?" he spat then stormed off. It seemed that I was totally incapable of saying the right thing that night. I also became aware of the fact that I may have been wrong with my initial opinion of the other pupils. Scratching beneath the surface revealed there were still some raw wounds twenty five years on.

My brother leaned towards me and whispered in my ear.

"See those men over there?" He pointed to a table in the corner where four men sat sombrely sipping their beers.

"Yeah."

"Don't you remember? All of them used to wet the bed, and here they are, twenty five years later, sitting with each other." I knew they found comfort in each other's company at school, but it still surprised me to notice the strange kinships that still applied years later. Two of the school bullies had sought each other out immediately and had reverted to type by going round the bar in a drunken state taking the piss out of the same people they intimidated back in school. Masks that they had spent years cultivating had slipped to reveal the insecure bully, the victim, the spectator and the Stonekicker. I wanted to leave but I was duty bound to spend the night there. I had often fantasised about what I would do as a grown man when confronted by the people that had made so many children's lives hell. God knows, the things I had experienced and the people I have had to deal with since leaving school had made me more than capable of teaching them all a thing or too. But I didn't. I no longer felt the need to carry out such acts of vengeance and repentance. The whole scene was pathetic; old men desperately trying to either reassert their authority or else denying to themselves that any of the crimes they had committed had ever happened. People needed to get on with their lives and ditch all of this baggage.

I stood at the bar for a while and was approached by Luke. He had lost most of his hair now and had put on a bit of weight around the middle.

"Hello Luke," I said. "Looking good."

"Yeah, right," he replied. "At least I don't look like

I've got leukaemia anymore. What have you been up to for the last twenty years then, stranger?" I told him. For a few years after leaving school we had kept in touch, going out clubbing at weekends. We eventually lost touch. I couldn't remember why.

"What about yourself?" I asked.

"I'm a machine setter in a factory," he said. "I've been there for fifteen years now. It isn't the best job in the world but it pays the bills." It occurred to me that nobody seemed to have set the world on fire in later life; in fact I'd heard that at least a dozen of the ex-pupils had actually done time in prison. Good job I'd managed to keep my chosen profession a secret.

"Sounds good," I lied. "You married?" I asked remembering his adolescent fumblings with Joe.

"Yeah, I've got six kids and counting," he said with forced enthusiasm then changed the subject immediately. Have you heard of Dungeons and Dragons?" he asked.

"Isn't that that kids' game?" I asked.

"Kids haven't got a bloody clue!" he said indignantly. "I am number nine in the country!" he exclaimed with pride, then launched into an extremely detailed account of what that entailed.

As the conversation ended I turned to Joe who was standing on the other side of me.

"Did you hear that?" I said.

"What?"

"He was telling me all about all this Dungeons and Dragons malarkey. I didn't have a clue what he was going on about."

"It's brilliant," said Joe. "He's in the top ten in the country. I've had a few goes myself. I've even made my own crossbow and have gone on some of the get-togethers with him. We've had a right laugh."

"Cool," I said. Oh, Jesus Christ get me out of here, I thought. The world had gone mad. I was feeling pretty depressed by then. The only people I had had any sort of a bond with had grown into aliens. I went back to join my brother.

At the end of the event on the way to the dormitory I passed a dozen or so old boys throwing each other into the pool. They were led by Clock. This group was one of the factions that revelled in being children again, people who, for a brief moment in time, forgot about the sorry lives they led working in factories or on the dole; people who would conveniently forget this behaviour along with the things they did at school when it came to disciplining their own children. They would frown upon any misdemeanours committed by their offspring insisting that they never behaved like that before administering a few sharp backhanders in the firm knowledge that it never did them any harm. Hypocrites. But what was I? Although I had grown up using my own experiences as a sort of code as to how *not* to behave, how not to treat children or loved ones, truly believing that I had managed to rise above it, I had still come here seeking revenge as well as atonement.

There was still a part of me that was that angry young boy fighting against the world and his dog; that still blamed this place for everything that had gone wrong in my life. But I also believed in a strange way that it was responsible for everything that had gone *right* in my life; that I needed to be allowed to learn to fight for myself at such a young age, making the mistakes I made along the road, to be able to face the world and see it for all of its flaws so that I would develop the tools necessary to combat the evils of the world in later life.

The next morning I awoke in the dormitory feeling very strange. It wasn't as I expected it to be. There was no pleasant nostalgia. I was hungry and wanted to go home. We walked down to the dining hall for breakfast. The Christians had been kind enough to let us use the facilities for the reunion but we still had to share it with them. The dining hall was full of kids with a handful of tables given to the ex-pupils at the bottom end of the hall. I sat down to eat my breakfast. There was instantly recognisable sound of a mug hitting a table to attract everybody's attention. I looked up to see a middle-aged man in combat trousers and a t-shirt that read 'Jesus Rocks'. He reminded me of the fuckers that used to visit the school every other Sunday when I was there.

"Morning kids," he shouted.

"Morning Kev," the kids yelled back.

"We're going to start this beautiful day with a song." He leaned forward and typed something into a laptop and the wall behind him lit up with the lyrics to a song. Music came from the speakers on the wall. The music was instantly recognisable as it came from a very popular hip-hop song that had recently had some chart success; the lyrics however had been changed to incorporate the word of God. I sat there in stunned silence as Kev started rapping about Jesus. All of the kids in the hall joined in, some standing and dancing, most tapping feet and fingers to the beat. It was a twenty-first century version of the crap that we had had to put up with all those years ago. Bitterness began to seep into my veins. I chuckled and it went away.

I spent the next couple of hours wandering around with my brother. We walked down the hill to the village and went into the local pub for a drink. A lot of the other ex-pupils and staff were there too. I didn't really fancy a pint but I couldn't resist the allure of drinking alcohol in front of people who would have flogged me into a bloody heap for drinking years before. Even though many years had passed I could see that they still saw us as children. They all, without exception carried with them an air of supercilious arrogance and probably inwardly seethed to see the pupils finally 'get on over on them'. What drew them to the reunion? That I couldn't figure. Was it to see if they still had what it took? Maybe. Redemption? I doubt it.

After an hour or so of chewing the fat with the old bastards as if nothing had ever happened I made my way home. On the drive back I was trying to decide whether or not I felt relieved that not one of the handful of real victims that I knew of, the kids whose lives were made hell every single day by pupils and teachers alike, hadn't made it to the reunion. There was no Slash, Rubbish or Windowlicker. I knew there were people there who had treated them worse than I had, but it would have been difficult looking them in the eye had they chosen to turn up. Maybe they hadn't heard about it. Maybe… well, there were more than a few reasons for them not to attend; reasons that I didn't care to dwell on.

Just as I was about to get into my car I spotted a six inch nail in the gutter. I picked it up and walked into the car park. I spotted Clock's car, glanced around to see that no-one was looking and wedged the nail between the road and Clock's car tyre. As I was driving out of the car park I spotted one of the teachers leaving the pub. I succeeded in fighting the urge to mow him down, but I did hit my horn as I passed him in the small hope of giving him a coronary.

I dropped my brother off at his house. "Thanks for coming along to that," I said. "Sorry if it was a bit shit."

"No need to apologise, he said. "I found it

fascinating. I can't believe you stuck that for five years."

"I didn't have a lot of say in the matter," I replied. We said our goodbyes and I drove home.

When I got home my daughters ran to greet me and lifted my spirits immediately. My wife was at the sink with her back to me. I grabbed an elastic band from my daughters' box of hair accessories and greeted her with a flick on the backside. She turned to me and shook her head in mock dismay.

"It's about time you grew up," she said.

The End

Made in the USA
Charleston, SC
09 April 2011